I0570596

LOVE OF THE GAME

THE GAMES WE PLAY

ANNA ZABO

LOVE OF THE GAME

ANNA ZABO

This is a work of fiction. Names, characters, places, and any incidents are either the product of the authors' imagination or are used fictitiously. Any resemblance to actual persons, living or dead, to business establishments, events, or locales is entirely coincidental.

Love of the Game

First Edition

Copyright © 2024 by Anna Zabo

Edited by Mackenzie Walton

Cover design by L. C. Chase

All rights reserved. No part of this book may be reproduced or transmitted in any form or by any means, electronic or mechanical, including photocopying, recording, or by any information storage and retrieval systems without written permission from the author, and where permitted by law. Reviewers may quote brief passages in a review.

Print ISBN: 978-1-947550-18-6

THE GAMES WE PLAY HOCKEY LEAGUES

- **NAPH** (North American Professional Hockey) - Major league.
- **PHL** (Professional Hockey League) - Minor league.
- **HLENA** and **HLWNA** (Hockey League of Eastern North America and the Hockey League of Western North America) - Second tier minor league

CONTENT NOTES

This book contains:

- Small instances of harassment from biological father
- Mentions of queerphobia, but no on-page instances
- Use of alcohol and scenes in a bar
- Mentions of betting (gambling)
- Explicit, on page sex
- Hockey fighting
- Injury
- Hospital visit
- Character on pain medication
- On-page mental therapy
- Hockey fights

CHAPTER 1

DRAKE

"Williams."

Oh man, I flinched at the tone of Coach Robinson's voice. Firm, with a hint that I wasn't going to enjoy what he had to say. Last time he'd spoken to me like this, he'd shuffled me from the first line to the third, and the next week, I'd been scratched entirely. I'd spent the last three games in the press box. Bet plenty of people were loving that.

I paused in my quest to strip off my gear from practice. "Yeah, Coach?" I was still pissed at myself for my play so far this year, idling in the press box, and the damn drills they'd run at practice today (I was not a PKer, for fuck's sake).

That frustration must've ended up in my voice, because he gave me a look that only a father of five could manage. "After you shower, JR wants to see you upstairs."

Oh *shit*. JR was Jeremy Roth, our general manager. Going upstairs usually meant being traded. It was early in the season, though—just after Thanksgiving—so who knew what this meant. I swallowed and nodded. Once I was cleaned and dressed, I headed up the stairs that led to the staff offices above the locker rooms, and knocked on the doorframe of the GM's office, my heart in my throat.

JR looked up from his laptop. "Drake. Come in and sit down, son."

Son. Fuck. I kept my mouth shut, and took a seat in front of his desk.

He folded his hands together. "This is never easy, so I'm not going to beat around the bush. We're placing you on waivers this afternoon."

Waivers? "What?" I choked out the word, then slammed my lips together before the *"Are you fucking kidding me?"* poured out. I was still on my entry level contract until the end of the season, but I'd been waivers-eligible for a while. Hell, I'd never played in the PHL. I'd come straight to the Lions camp from the draft, made the team, and never left.

Now, I was likely off to some other NAPH team, slump or not. I was too good to end up in the PHL. Right?

Are you? That tiny voice in my head was awfully loud, and a certain set of direct messages flashed through my mind's eye.

JR sighed. "I hate to do this, son, believe me. But the team's in a slump, and so are you. We're bringing up some fresh faces. Shake some things up a bit. Hopefully, you'll find your game again with the Otters."

The Greensburg Otters were the affiliate of the Pitts-burgh Lions. They were only an hour away, but they might as well have been on the West Coast for all I paid attention to them. "You—think I'll clear?" That chilled me to my marrow. Was I so bad now that no other NAPH team would take a chance on me?

I don't know if he was actually calculating in his head, or just playing the thoughtful manager, but after a moment, he straightened in his seat. "It's hard to know how it'll go. We'd prefer for you to stay in the system—you're a good player when you're on your game, Drake."

I wasn't on my game. Hadn't been, despite blowing it out of the water in training camp. I had no idea what the fuck was wrong with me, and now suddenly, I had to prove myself. Two years of effort and good play wasn't enough. "I guess—I guess I should pack my stuff up." I was going somewhere tomorrow, regardless. Question now was where.

He nodded and rose. "Like I said, son. We'd rather you stay in the system, find your game, and come back and play like you have in the past. Sometimes a change of scenery helps."

Personally, if I had to choose—since I couldn't stay here —I wanted another NAPH team to claim me. I had to believe I was still a good player in a slump not... useless. I shut down that thought, rose and shook JR's hand. "I guess we'll see. I like it here."

That was the truth. Pittsburgh was kind of the perfect hockey town. Big city enough, but not so much that it was unbearable. And my entry-level salary went pretty far.

I headed back down to the locker room to pack up my equipment and talk to the logistics people about moving— either temporarily or permanently. My God, if I ended up with the Otters, I was royally fucked. I'd be making a tenth of what I made now there. How the hell would I pay the rent on my downtown apartment? I'd still need it for when —if—the Lions called me up.

Shit. Fuck. This was so stupid, all of it. If I hadn't been sitting in the fucking press box— Then again, I was sitting there because in eighteen games, I had one assist, no goals, and was a minus 10. Shit season. Shit play. *Useless.* There was that word again.

No wonder they were waiving me.

When I got back to the locker room, it was completely empty, except for Bearsy—Kevin Bear—our team captain. He had a fucking look of pity on his face.

"Guess you heard," I said.

"Yeah." He stretched out his legs. "You'll be all right, Duck. And look, if you end up going to the Otters, there's some great guys down there. And you'll be back soon enough, if you do end up down."

Ugh. I did not want to end up on the Otters. "I hate leaving. No matter where I end up. I wish—" Yeah, I wished a lot of things. I gave Bearsy a shrug. "Well, can't do anything about it now."

He clapped me on the shoulder. "I'll see you around, eh?"

Yeah. Maybe. Hopefully.

Fuck. I was getting *waived*.

Didn't take too long to pack up my gear and grab my sticks. Back in my apartment I ordered food, then paced my living room, and tried to figure out what the hell to do next. It wasn't two o'clock yet. I knew once the news came out, my phone would be barraged with texts.

Phone. Right. I took a deep breath, then called my mom. My sperm donor would laugh when he found out, the fucker, but my mom had busted her ass to make sure I could make it in hockey. She shouldn't find out I was being waived from the internet.

"Hey sweetie, what's up?"

I couldn't keep the tremble out of my voice. "Mom, they're waiving me."

"Oh, honey!" she murmured. "It's okay."

I sighed. "I mean, I know I haven't been playing well, and I've been scratched but..."

"You're just in a slump, that all!" She paused, and added, "Maybe a change of place will be a good thing. A new city."

Assuming another NAPH team wanted me. With the way I'd started the year? Who knew what they thought. "Coach said they'd love to keep me in the system. But if I end up down with the Otters..." I heaved a sigh of my own. "It's a lot less money."

"Hmm," Mom said, "You've been putting away some of your salary, right? Like the advisor said?"

"Of course." First thing Mom suggested I'd get when I'd signed my contract at nineteen was a financial advisor. "I have savings. I just hate tapping into it."

"Well, maybe it won't come to that." She sounded so sure. "Either way, at least you'll be out of the press box, right? Playing again?"

Trust Mom to find the bright side of things. I laughed humorlessly. "Yeah, I guess."

We chatted a little longer, the conversation moving from my impending doom to her job as an accountant, then news about some of the kids I'd grown up with. Who was getting married, who was still living in our little suburban Philly town, and who'd moved on to other things. Emily, one of Mom's neighbor's daughters, was doing really well in med school and Jaxson, a boy I'd had a bunch of fights with, then kissed once, had graduated from college with a degree in economics and was apparently dating a drama major.

It was supposed to make me feel better, but it only served to remind me that I, who'd been drafted in the first round (albeit last), and had played lights out my first and second year in the NAPH, was about to go through waivers because my team didn't want me anymore. Because I sucked.

By the time I hung up with Mom, I was more than a little depressed. Part of me wanted to say, "Fuck it" and go head out to one of my favorite restaurants in town, have a huge meal, and get totally smashed. The other part of me wanted to fire up a hookup app and find a guy to fuck until my mind was numb.

What I did instead was trudge to my closet to pack.

AT TWO-FIFTEEN, SLIGHTLY TWENTY-FOUR HOURS after I'd been placed on waivers, Bearsy texted me.

> Yo, Duck, glad you're sticking around in the area. Pretty sure you'll be up again before the new year. Give Jonny a call. He's the captain. He'll take care of you.

That was followed with a phone number with an 878-area code. I rolled my eyes and tossed my phone onto the couch. Lot of good a new captain would do me. I was done.

Every other team in the league had passed over me. No one wanted me. I was heading to the minors. I knew that this had been a possibility, maybe even likely, but now that the minutes had ticked past the deadline and I cleared waivers, the reality set in.

A complete gut punch, one that had my eyes stinging and my stomach roiling. I was now a Greensburg Otter, with a paycheck ninety percent smaller than before. As my mom had reminded me, I was fine financially, for a good long while, but it still fucking hurt.

In theory, I didn't even have to move. Right now, it took me about twenty minutes to get to the Lions practice facility, and Greensburg was only an hour away.

But I knew it would be easier if I lived closer to Greensburg because that commute wasn't always an hour, especially considering the Squirrel Hill Tunnel and the ever-present construction on the roads between here and there. Add other drivers to that mix, and I was looking at a long daily commute.

Fuck. My phone dinged again. This text was from Lions staff, connecting me up with Otters staff. Emails followed with more details I skimmed over. I was expected for practice tomorrow at the Westmoreland Arena at ten in the morning. They suggested a hotel nearby as a temporary place to stay, at least for a few days. There was also a list of short-term rentals in the area. Some other things about the team, the coach, and the leadership.

More texts from the Otters coach welcoming me. One from their captain. I ignored those. Couldn't stomach reading through the rest of it, not with my eyes blurring.

I was going to the minors because *no one wanted me.* That thought kept circling through my head. It was all my fault. Maybe if I'd played better... Maybe if I'd practiced harder... Or maybe it was a damn fluke I was even ever drafted into the NAPH in the first place.

I'd had to block my sperm donor on Instagram. Hell, I shut down direct messages entirely, since my mother, teammates, and friends all texted, but some of the shit he'd said when he'd found me still ate at me.

I rubbed at my eyes. Okay, fine. I was here, now. First, get a hotel. Second, get the hell out of here before I had a breakdown.

A little under three hours later, I was checking into a Marriott on the edge of a strip mall on the outskirts of Greensburg.

Fuck my life. This box of a room would be home for...

however long it took to unfuck myself, I guess. Or until the Lions traded me.

Great... just...

I sat on the bed and searched for the closest gay bar. Yeah, I had practice tomorrow, but I needed a drink or three and a nice hard fuck, ASAP. It was a risk—get too far out of Pittsburgh, and the surrounding area got more conservative, but a long time ago, I realized there were queer people everywhere. And with Greensburg being a college town, there was likely some queer-friendly bar nearby, right? A little searching around in the right places netted me a good lead for what someone described as an eclectic queer-friendly biker bar tucked into where you'd least expect it in the hills between Jeanette and Greensburg. Sounded like it was worth at least a drive to check out.

Took me a little bit to find the place, aptly named the Hideaway. It really was in a location where you'd least expect it—off a road that was far away from any of the major ones, tucked between what looked like a dirt driveway that led back to a farm and a business that rented construction equipment.

The place didn't look like much from the outside—a dive bar with some cars and several motorbikes out front, but there was a rainbow flag hanging in the window next to some actual neon signs advertising different brands of beer, so this had to be the right bar. I parked my SUV next to an older Ford pickup and got out.

I didn't know motorcycles well, but I knew enough to identify a Harley, all black and chrome, parked close to the entrance. The interior of the bar was decorated like a tidy version of a garage that was the child of a leather daddy and a unicorn. Chrome, leather, tools, mirrors, bike parts, and rainbows. Somehow it worked. Quite a few people, more than I expected for a Tuesday night, were gathered. Some around the bar, a few in booths, and several around the two pool tables in the back.

Everyone was watching me, which was understandable. Local bar. Off the beaten path. I was a stranger, though apparently not threatening, because the two men in full biker leathers and club jackets nodded at me and went back to their conversation.

I wasn't about to mess with them. I wasn't here to mess with anyone. A drink had been my first goal, so I headed to the bar—and nearly stumbled over my own feet when I met the gaze of a man sitting there.

Goddamned, he was a looker. Dark brown hair and eyes accentuated by pale skin, a goatee, and a devilish smile. He looked like a dark version of a fox.

Trying to recover, I stammered, "Guess you don't get new people coming in that often."

That got me an even wider grin, one that lit up those eyes and set them dancing. His voice was clear when he answered. "Well, it's not rare, but let's stay it's unexpected." He patted the bar stool next to him.

I took the invitation to sit, and the bartender, a Black woman with braids and a name tag that read Ella, strode up. "You sure he's old enough to be in here, Jon?"

"Eh, he's a little baby-faced," the smoking hot guy replied. "But I bet he's old enough." The smile never diminished.

"I'm twenty-two." Nearly twenty-three. My cheeks heated. Yeah, I looked a little young. Didn't help that I was fair and blond and my stubble was barely visible most of the time. "I have ID, if you need to see it."

The man—Jon—waved his hand as if to say, *You see?*

She rolled her eyes at Jon. "You know I have to check

their ID if they look under thirty. You want this place to get busted?"

Jon rolled his eyes right back.

I showed her my driver's license and she gave me a small smile. "What'll you have?"

"Beer. Whatever's local, good, and can help me put a bad day behind me."

She chuckled. "I got you. Hang on, babyface."

While she poured me a beer, I checked Jon out. Fuck me, he was in really good shape. The white T-shirt he wore stretched over muscles, and colorful tattooed sleeves snaked up both arms, vanishing beneath the bright fabric to peek out at the collar of his shirt. There was even ink on the back of his right hand, but I couldn't make out the design. He wore jeans and leather chaps, and I was glad I'd worn my slightly looser jeans, because this man was straight out of my wet dreams.

Well, hopefully *not* straight.

Still, I didn't need to be tenting my pants like a teenager. "Hey, I'm Drake."

"Drake? Like a dragon?"

I had to laugh. "Well, that's better than Drake, like a duck."

That smile again. "You look more like a dragon than a duck." He turned to Ella as she brought me a beer. "He looks more like a dragon than a duck, right?"

Ella gave him a look that I suspected she'd cast his way several hundred times. "He looks thirsty. Leave the boy to his drink."

He clicked his tongue. "I'm harmless."

I nearly inhaled the beer, then met his wicked, wicked grin as I tried not to choke.

Ella snorted and dropped a pile of cocktail napkins in

front of me. "Sure you are, Jon." Then she sauntered down the bar.

He laughed as I recovered my breath and took an actual sip of the beer. Good pick—not too hoppy, and with a depth of flavors that I didn't expect in this area of Pennsylvania. "Oh, that'll do."

"So, Drake like a dragon, what brings you here?" There was a curiosity there that read genuine, like he actually wanted to know. Everything about Jon was open and free. Cheerful rather than smarmy.

"Work." Then I amended. "Well, not *here* here. I found this place hunting for a queer bar. Here as in the area."

He rounded his mouth in a silent "o" before it settled back into that seemingly ever-present smile. "So not here for the bikes?"

I laughed. "I've never driven one. I guess I was hoping for a different ride. Maybe not tonight, but sometime." I paused and wrapped a hand around my glass and sighed. "It's been a fucking *day*." I took another sip.

Jon was halfway through his beer and took a pull from his glass as if he intended to nurse the remainder. He licked those pretty lips of his, then said, "I'm guessing the same work that brings you here is the one that's made it a day?"

"Yeah." I sighed and tried to figure out how to say what I wanted without letting on that I was a hockey player. "It's... not a demotion at work. More like... temporarily moving to a different office. A change of scenery. But honestly, I don't want to be here." I paused. "I'm sure Greensburg is nice enough, but all my stuff is back in Pittsburgh, just far away enough to make commuting really difficult." I rotated my beer glass. "In some ways, moving across country would've been easier."

He cocked his head. "For a temporary assignment? I'd

think it would be easier to be close to home. You could go home on weekends. See family."

"No family nearby."

He made another "o" with those inviting lips of his. "So, all alone in a queer bar somewhere you don't want to be?" His tone was soft and friendly, and that perpetual smile real. He was... gorgeous. Relaxed.

But his words itched at me. "When you put it that way, it sounds kind of bad..."

"No, I mean—" He picked up his glass and waved it at the bar. "People not from the area usually come here for one or two things. A drink." He clinked his glass against mine. "Or a fuck." He sipped and watched me. "Or both."

I scratched the back of my neck, embarrassment once more creeping up my spine. "I'm guessing the answer to the second thing is 'No, kid.'"

The smile returned. "You're not a kid. And it takes two dates to ride this ride."

"So there's a chance?"

He laughed, and it was high and wonderful and weird, and everyone in the bar must have heard it.

What really got me was the joy in his face. I'd never understood how people could be so damn... happy... all the time. I'd only known Jon a few minutes, and he made my heart race, seeing all that happiness. I wanted some of that, some of *him*.

He sobered a bit, but didn't drop that sense of enjoying the hell out of everything. "Why don't you come back here tomorrow night and ask me that?"

The Otters had a game tomorrow. Shit. "I have to work pretty late. I know the bar's open but..." I trailed off.

He waved my concern away. "I'll be here, promise. Don't you worry about that."

That had me giving him a once-over. "For me?"

What a fucking grin. "Yes." Then I swear his eyes freaking twinkled, as he added, "And for me, too. I love this place."

Ella walked by and smacked Jon lightly on the back of the head. "You own this place."

"Well, yes. But that's why I bought it from Frank when he wanted to retire. Because I loved it." He shrugged. "It was either that or he was going to close it, and I didn't want that to happen."

I looked around the place, with its patrons of all genders, and the rough-looking bikers, including the two who had entered while I was taking the place in—wearing jackets emblazoned with their motorcycle club. They nodded to Jon as they passed us, and saddled up to the bar, chatting freely with Ella.

"This does seem a special place," I said.

That seemed to please Jon. "Oh, it is. When I first came here—" He cut himself off with a laugh. "That's probably a story for another night. Let's just say it's been good to me, so I decided to try to be good to it, and everyone around here."

A group of four women headed over from one of the two pool tables— two couples from the way they were holding each other. One of them patted Jon on the shoulder. "See you tomorrow night, Jonny?"

"Absolutely," he said, then added that big smile of his.

She gave me a curious once over, but she and her group moved on, heading for the door.

"Hey." He tapped his shoe against mine. "You play?" He nodded toward the vacated pool table.

"A little. One of the guys has a table in his house and sometimes..." I waved my hand, because it hurt to think about those get-togethers. Those parties. I just been celebrating Thanksgiving with the Lions. Christmas was around the corner, and I was...here. In the middle of nowhere. At a bar. With no friends or teammates around me.

Jon tapped my foot again, and those deep dark eyes met mine, with all their sparkle and laugh lines. "Come on. I'm absolutely horrible. It'll be fun! You can laugh at me."

I sighed. I should go back to the hotel, but I hadn't even finished my beer. "Okay. A game." I asked Ella for a glass of water to go with my beer, and we headed back to the table.

Jon was being honest about his skill at pool. His break shot—well—it didn't really do much other than move the balls a little bit from their original racked position.

"Hmm," he said. "Maybe we should try that again and you break?"

We did, and I managed a reasonable break shot. Jon potted a solid ball, and I managed two easy stripes. Then we took turns missing shots or sending balls wild or knocking each other's into the pockets. Jon was hilarious, chattering away with a running commentary about his shots, his expressions and exasperation at his inability to sink the balls was comical, and his smile was pure sunlight.

Despite being not great at pool, I won easily, and by the end, I'd finished my beer and my water, and even felt some of the weight of the day lifting off me.

As we headed back to the bar, I hazarded a light pat on his back. "Thanks for the game."

"And the beer," he said.

When I started to protest, he waved that away. "On the house, don't you worry. The owner's a bit of a jerk, though. Don't tell him." Then he winked. Actually winked at me.

An actual chuckle squeaked out of me. "I won't." I

paused by where we'd been sitting—the bikers were still there, talking—and faced Jon. "Was that a date?"

"Ha!" He clapped me on the shoulder. "Come back tomorrow night and ask me that."

So maybe yes, maybe no. But it felt like that chance was better, now.

Maybe this place wouldn't be horrible after all.

CHAPTER 2

JON

I pondered the door to the bar Drake Williams had left through, and wondered what the others thought of the center the Lions had sent down for us to un-fuck. And contemplated how I wanted to fuck him.

Such a bad idea, but oh, I bet it would be a such a *good* time.

"He's going to kill you tomorrow," Ella said. "Though, I can't believe he didn't recognize you."

I shrugged. "Oh, come on. It's not like I'm famous, or even well known outside of the area." Sure, I was the captain of the Otters, but that and a dollar would get me a really crappy hot dog on dollar dog nights at the arena.

"Jonny." Red Dog rotated on his stool, which set his leather jacket creaking. "That kid is trouble. He's not gonna help you boys at all."

I rolled his words around in my head. Red Dog was the president of the Night Bones MC. I wasn't a member of any club, but Red Dog hadn't gotten to his position by lacking intelligence, so I respected and listened, as one should to elders.

"No, you're right, he's not here to help. We're supposed to help him. That's why he was sent down." I sat on the stool next to him and his deputy, Merrick, and broke one of my own rules—started talking hockey in the bar. Red Dog would understand, though. This was a serious talk, not bar chatter. "He's got skills, obviously. We all saw what he did his first two years."

"Crashed and burned this year," Red Dog said. "You think he can come back from that?"

I rocked my head, trying to decide if that was true. "It's still early enough in the season. Bearsy says the kid's trying too hard. All the issues are up here." I tapped my head.

"Oh lord," Ella muttered. "And they sent him to *you* to fix?"

Merrick chuckled and took a swig of his beer.

"Oh, come on, I'm not that bad."

Ella lifted one eyebrow and stared at me. Red Dog side-eyed me.

"I'm not!"

Now all three were looking at me, all dubiously. Ella spoke first. "Jon, do you think getting into that boy's pants is going to help him be a better hockey player?"

I shrugged again, and Red Dog sighed. "Jonny..."

I held up my hands. "I'm not out to fuck him." Not really. It wasn't a good idea. Not good at all. "And yes, I think I can help. He'd got a chip on his shoulder."

"Your dick's not gonna knock that off," Merrick muttered.

"Oh, it might, you never know." I held up my hands again when Red Dog gave me his withering look.

"Lord," Ella said. "Save me from this fool of a man."

"God's not that kind," Red Dog said.

"Hey, it's not like I go out of my way to sleep with teammates."

Ella scoffed and threw her rag down on the counter. "That fool Adam accidentally fell on your dick then?"

I winced. You'd think after three years, people would forget about that, but alas. "Adam was a—mistake. Pretty—but a mistake." Adam Darelo, a sandy-haired left-shooting defenseman with lovely hazel eyes, had lasted three-quarters of a season on the Otters before he'd been traded. Playing-wise, he'd had sparks of—something—on occasion, but was mediocre otherwise. He'd been so fun in bed, though. Just—vibrant and enthusiastic. The Adam whirlwind had been great, right up until I'd discovered he'd also railed his way through the less-than-straight part of the team. Not so great for the married guys, or those with partners. Half the team ended up a snarling mess. Cleaning up after that disaster had been something.

"That's why I have the dating rule," I said. "And tonight doesn't count as a date."

"*Sure* it doesn't," Merrick said.

"It doesn't." I think the lack of mirth in my voice might have finally convinced them I was being serious, because all three watched me carefully. "I won't lie and say I'm not attracted to him or that I don't want him, but Drake's got to get whatever's in his head worked out. While a good roll in the sheets *might* help with that, I have the team to think about."

Red Dog nodded. "You have to consider what's best for the club." The Night Bones could be a hell of a lot more selective about their members, and the buck stopped with Red Dog. Not so with me. I might be captain, but the buck stopped a hell of a lot higher up on the food-chain.

"I don't make the personnel decisions. But the team is still mine."

"And now Drake William is an Otter," Ella said.

Which meant he, too, was mine, at least as far as that went. The Lions would call him up eventually, if he unfucked his head. There was time to see what the best approach would be in helping with that. Flirting tonight hadn't hurt that. And yeah, Drake would probably be mad, but what happened after that would tell me more than anything else would.

But as I told my friends—I wanted him. That, I couldn't deny. More than that—I really did want to help Drake.

He was a hell of a better player than me, but the stress and sadness and frustration in that man... I shook my head. "Well, tomorrow's another day, yeah?" I beamed at the two bikers and my bartender. "If nothing else, it'll be interesting!"

———

ALAS, OVERNIGHT, THE WEATHER TURNED TO COLD rain from the brisk but dry late fall, so I pulled my old truck rather than my bike into the players lot at the arena. None of the other players were here yet, which wasn't unusual. Coach Macintosh's truck was, along with the SUVs of some of the other training staff.

Mac caught up with me in the locker room as he breezed through. "Hey, Jonny. That kid from the Lions is arriving today. You good with taking him under your wing?"

"Absolutely. You know I'm always willing to help."

Mac grunted. "I've been studying film. No idea what the issue is. He's talented. Played his ass off for two years.

And now..." He shrugged and jawed his gum. "Got any ideas?"

"Some," I said, and beamed at Mac. Though I bet pissing Drake off inadvertently was not what Mac had in mind.

He rolled his eyes. "You behave yourself, Jonny boy. This kid's gonna be a star if he can get it turned around."

Mac was usually right about his talent estimations. Drake *had* been burning it up before this season. I headed over to the fitness room so I could warm my legs up on the bike. "I promise I'll be good."

"Jon." Mac said my name with a gruffness I recognized, so I halted in the doorway and met his gaze. "Yeah, Coach?"

He gave me one of those knowing looks, and I wondered what I'd given away. I swear, Mac could read our minds. "You got something you want to tell me?" he asked.

After a couple of years being coached by Mac, I knew better than to shrug his concern off. "He stopped by the bar last night but didn't recognize me, that's all."

Mac groaned. "Don't tell me you hit on him."

"Other way around, actually. He came in looking for a drink and a..." I waved my hand. "Ride."

Mac squeezed his eyes shut and pinched his nose. "Jonny, you're supposed to be the *responsible* one of you nutballs."

"I didn't do anything! We talked. Played pool. He went back to... well, his hotel, I suppose."

"And? Because there's a point to this long story of yours. There always is."

It wasn't that long of a story, I didn't think, but I held up my hands to placate Mac. "Okay, okay. Point is, he didn't know who I was. Still doesn't know."

"Oh," Mac said, then paused, probably because the whole issue behind my words sank in. "*Oh*. Huh."

"I know I'm asking a lot in this situation and maybe my way isn't the most orthodox for integrating a player, but do you trust me?"

He paced a small circle in the locker room and rubbed his chin. "I have no idea how your brain works, Jonny. Kid's going to be super pissed at you. But I'll let you handle it." He stopped, then pinned me with a stare. "For now."

"Two games," I said. "Give me two games to get him into the team."

He held up two fingers. "Better work, Jonny boy."

I nodded and kept my mouth closed.

Mac waved me away. "Go do your thing."

I spun and quickly made for one of the bikes in the fitness room. Helped get my legs going. I'd turn thirty on January 5—not old yet, but age was starting to catch up with me. By the time I finished and returned to the locker room, the other guys were filtering in. Clancy, our goalie, was in his quiet zone, earbuds in as he got his mountain of gear on. Hardy and Lou, though, were their normal gregarious selves. "So we're getting Drake Williams, huh? Not had a great year so far."

"Happens sometimes," I said. "It'll be fine. He's got good wheels and hands, just has had some bad luck. We can get him back on his feet. We're here to help the big club, you know?"

There was a cough at the doorway, and there stood Drake in his base layer, with Hank White, our equipment manager. "Guys, this is Drake Williams. Drake, your stall is over there, next to the captain, Jonny Eriksson."

Drake's eyes narrowed when that fiery gaze met mine,

and his jaw tensed, but that was the only tell that he was fuming at me. "Great," he said.

Hank set down Drake's hockey bag on the floor next to me. "The Lions sent down the specs on your gear, so I got a bunch of things ready for you, but holler if you need anything in particular."

His shoulders relaxed a bit. "Thanks—Hank, right?"

Hank nodded, patted Drake on the back, and left him to us.

Drake sat down with a huff onto the bench next to me. His eyes cut my way, still full of fire. "Jonny, huh? So you're the captain?"

"I am." I beamed at him. "Welcome to the Greensburg Otters."

He unzipped his duffle and started pulling out his protective gear. "Not just a bar owner then."

Hardy whistled at that just as Lou said, "Uh oh."

Me? I laughed. Couldn't help it. Then I smiled at Drake. "Oh, I'm that, too." Then I added, "I think we're going to call you Dragon. You're *really* not a Duck. No idea what those guys were thinking when they named you that." I shook my head. "Not a good nickname."

Drake paused, jock in hand, and stared at me.

"You don't mind Dragon, do you?"

His brow was full of creases. Some from frustration, but the confusion there had taken the edge off that. "No."

"Oh good, that's settled then!" I strapped my shin and knee guards on. Followed those with my socks, standing to clip those into the garters.

"It's two syllables," Hardy said.

"So's your mom," Lou replied, and Hardy smacked him.

"Jonny's two syllables," I said. "I had a perfectly good one syllable name and you all had to make it longer. And anyway, Sandwich"—I poked my thumb at Lou—"is also two syllables."

Hardy waved my words away. "Eh, whatever." A beat passed. "Jhonnnieee."

I snickered. "Better than Hard, don't you think?"

"Yeah," Lou chimed in. "I am not making a 'your mom' joke out of that, thanks, Cap."

For his part, Drake silently put on his gear while we chattered around him. Once he donned the Otters practice jersey, he finally spoke to me again. His words were quiet but still sharp, and they slipped beneath the noise in the room. "You could've told me who you were."

"Yeah, I could've." I plopped my helmet onto my head. Didn't bother with the chinstrap. "Admittedly, that probably was the easier path. But I had my reasons."

The frustration crept back into his voice and body. "Which are?"

I chuckled and tapped the plastic that encased my noggin. "Think about it for a little bit." I clapped him on the shoulder, then headed out of the room to grab my sticks and hit the ice.

———

Despite having a game that evening, Mac worked us at a high-energy pace at practice. We'd blown the previous game—mostly lack of details—so he had us battling along the boards and working both on breakouts and defending against the rush. Drake slotted in at center on the second line, and everyone on the ice could tell he didn't want to be here. His effort was... not great. Mac talked quietly with him a couple of times, as did the other coaches.

Drake nodded politely, discussed the finer points of the drills, then—just didn't go for it.

It was one of the new young guys—Alfie Joelsson, a winger from Sweden—who was the first to vent to me. "I trained with him in camp. Not that he remembers. He looked right through me when I said hi." Alfie shook his head in frustration, then switched to Swedish. "But what pisses me off is that he's got amazing hands and legs and IQ, and he's half-assing everything out there! No wonder they sent him down and called Gavin up."

Gavin Lacey was one of the other new guys—drafted last year and one of those Canadian born and bred hockey players. He wasn't as good as Drake Williams, but he had something that our new grumpy, frustrated dragon didn't have at the moment: determination.

"He needs time," I told Alfie. "And a little shift in his neurons, I think."

"I don't understand what happened. He was great his first two years."

Alfie's sentiment was a common refrain and one I was starting to wonder, too. Drake didn't say anything to the guys he'd been in camp with. He didn't really say anything to anyone, but you'd think he'd at least acknowledge the guys he'd met.

I hadn't been invited to the Lions camp for years, mostly because I was on a PHL contract now, so I'd never get a call-up, but partly because I asked them not to after the first two years. I was a *lot*. Bearsy called me Guy Smiley because I was this, as he put it, happy chatterbox who was always going. The boys loved me, but I didn't want to be a distraction, especially once it was certain I'd never play in the NAPH again.

The Otters were my team, my home. I was still a chatterbox here, still smiling, but I was part of the fabric of this team, even with its rotating cast of characters.

And now Drake Williams was here with his sad blue eyes, pretty blond curls, and fucked-up attitude. It was one thing to not know who I was, but some of these kids—he'd spent two weeks working with them.

Mike Smith (we called him Bike, partly because he'd sometime show up to practice on his bicycle and partly for... other reasons) muttered at me while we waited for our turn in a drill. "Fuck that dude."

Oh, I still wanted to.

Bad thought. No good. Needed to keep a lid on that. "Was he like this in camp?"

Bike shook his head. "Nah. He was serious and hard working. But he talked to us, you know? Helped with the drills. Not like—" He waved as Drake went through the motions of another power play drill with little effort. Mac blew the whistle, then barked at Drake to do it again. "That."

There was Alfie's question again. Whatever had happened had been between training camp and the start of the season. Or early on.

I stuffed that to the back of my mind as my turn with the drills came along. Mac used me on both the power play and the penalty kill, so he kept me busy. My hockey IQ was pretty good, which helped when it came to knowing where openings would appear or where pucks would come from, so I tended to be in the right place at the right time. At least down here. Up in the NAPH? Not so much. The game was a hell of a lot faster and I was...not. Never had been.

But years watching my dad play had helped the brain. I

understood the game, but I didn't have the hands or legs of a hall-of-famer. What I did have was an absolute love for everything hockey. The sounds, the sights, even the smell. I never wanted to leave the rink.

Drake had the hands and the legs and the IQ, but he looked miserable right now.

Practice went on with more drills, and I caught him watching me when I paused to catch my breath in between stints. Oh, he was still angry, given the narrowing of his eyes and frown when I caught him looking. But there was more there, too.

Hardy muttered, "I can't decide if he wants to kill you or fuck you."

"Could be both," I replied.

He snorted. "I can guess which one you want."

I rolled my eyes and shoved Hardy. But there were those bad thoughts again—the ones that ended up with Drake under me. Or on top of me. I wasn't that picky, really. There were no rules about teammates fraternizing, as long as screwing didn't screw the team, but the whole shit with Adam had kept me from doing anything more than harmlessly flirting with some of the guys. All air, no heat.

If I wanted a good tumble in the sheets, I could find that at the bar. What I really wanted with Drake was to see him smile. On the ice. Preferably after scoring a goal or three.

Yeah, and I wanted that smile in my bed, too.

Team first. Drake's future first. My libido could wait.

Drake didn't look any happier when Mac blew the whistle to end practice and gathered us all in.

"Tonight's going to be a fun one, boys. The Gators are tough and hungry and they need the points as much as we do. I expect you all to show up, work hard, and have fun." He gave the ice a tap with his stick. "Be here by five."

After Mac left, we all stretched out at center ice. Some left after that—Drake was one of those—and some of us stayed out to work on shooting. My one-timers had been missing the net more than hitting, so I worked with Lou for a while to recalibrate myself.

By the time I got into the locker room, the grumpy dragon was gone. By the time I got showered and dressed, I'd received word to talk to Mac before heading home. I went to his office, pausing to rap on the open door. "You wanted to see me?"

He pointed at the chair in front of his desk, and my heart did the flip it always did. Sitting down with your coach or your GM—that could be good or it could be bad or nothing at all, and I'd been through all the iterations.

I gestured to the door. "Open or..."

Mac glanced at the door. "You can leave it open."

Well, that meant it wasn't going to be too horrible a talk. I lowered myself into the guest chair. "I'm all yours."

He smiled and grunted. "I doubt that."

Heat touched my cheeks and I clamped my lips closed to stop from stuttering out a bunch of nonsense.

Mac snorted and shook his head. "You deserved that."

"Okay, yes. Probably." I took a breath. "But you're our coach and married and..." I bit off my words with a little *eep* as he raised an eyebrow at me.

"Straight?"

I shrugged. And kept my mouth shut. I was too busy swallowing my pride. And my Pride.

After letting me shift in my seat, he shook his head again. "I called you in here to talk about Drake Williams."

I cleared my throat. "Okay. Yeah. Drake. What about him?"

"You actually think you can work some kind of miracle with that kid? He absolutely does not want to be here."

"I know," I said. "And yes." I didn't know Drake, but there'd been something in those blue eyes that had drawn me in last night. And a joy buried underneath all that anger and sadness and frustration. "But it's probably not going to go well tonight, I don't think."

"No shit." Mac leaned back in his chair. "And I'm going to handle it like I always do."

Which meant limited ice time. You had to earn it in this club. Come to think of it, that was true for the Lions, too, which explained Drake's demotion. "Good," I said.

Mac watched me. "You like him."

Yeah, I kind of did. "I want to make him smile," I muttered. "That's all."

"Oh my God, Jonny." Mac picked a pen up off his desk, then tossed it back down.

"What's wrong with that? He looks so unhappy." Unhappy players played shitty hockey. Everyone knew that.

Mac studied me, entirely like I suppose a father might—but not my father. My papa would smile, wave, and tell me to get to it. Mostly because Papa never wanted me the kind of unhappy I thought might be eating at Drake. Mac, though—I suspected he thought I just wanted in Drake's pants or something.

Which I did. But not yet. I gave Mac my best puppy-dog eyes. "Trust me?"

He snorted. "You're wearing the C, Jonny. I trust you. But don't make me regret that, yeah?"

"Yes, Coach."

He waved at his door. "Go home and take a nap."

I nodded, then retreated the hell out of there. The drive

home soothed me, to an extent, but I never could nap before games. I always itched to go. I just fucking loved being out there.

And tonight's game promised to be very interesting indeed.

CHAPTER 3

DRAKE

Oh my God, this sucked. I sucked. Everything sucked. I sat on the bench, gripping my stick so tight, it was a wonder I didn't snap it. Halfway through the first period, I put my helmeted head down on the edge of the boards in front of me and hoped that maybe the universe would swallow me whole.

It did not. Instead, Jonny Eriksson's voice sounded in my ear. "Hey." Then he rubbed circles onto my back. "Breathe. It'll be okay."

I lifted my head and checked the scoreboard. The Gators were still up two goals to our none—two goals that my shitastic play had caused in the first five minutes of the game. Coach Macintosh had benched me after that, running shifts with eleven forwards rather than twelve. It was a non-subtle way of telling me I fucked up big time and couldn't be trusted on the ice. "We're losing. Because of me."

"Yeah, I know. It happens." I could practically hear the smile in his voice. "That'll change." He nudged me. "Look."

I focused on the action in the defensive end—near our

goaltender. An Otters D-man and one of the forwards (I hardly knew anyone's names) were battling against Gators players along the boards. The puck came free and right to the tape of another Otters forward, then the team was breaking out of their zone and heading up the ice for a three on one rush. A few seconds later, the puck was in the back of the Gators' net, and I was on my feet along with the rest of the bench and the crowd as the goal horn sounded and the goal song blared out around us.

"See?" Jon said. He put one arm around me as we leaned out to give our teammates fist-bumps. "Atta boy, Lou! That's the way to do it, guys!" he called out.

When I sat, before Coach sent Jon's line over the boards for a faceoff, I got a full view at that beaming smile of his. "You know, you said 'we'." Then he was gone, and I sat there, stunned.

I'd said "we." Our team. The Otters. The guys I'd let down. "I'm such a fuckup," I muttered.

The player who'd taken Jon's place on the bench gave me a quizzical look. He was familiar, but I couldn't quite— then it hit me. Training camp. Kid from Sweden. Had just come over. Was down in the minors to get used to the change in rink size. I couldn't remember his name.

Fuck me, I really was a jackass.

But being down only one goal felt less hopeless than two. And by the time the period ended, Jon had been correct. The Otters—my team—had tied the game. Back to a clean slate. Mostly.

In the locker room, Coach gave a quick speech about sticking to our game and playing simple with attention to details. I swear he looked at me when he said that, or maybe that was my guilty conscience. Afterward, Jon handed me a sports drink, despite me spending most of the period riding the bench. I gave him a look, and he shrugged. "You'll need it for next period."

"You think Coach is going to put me in?"

Fuck, that grin of his. "Oh yeah. He will, to see how you respond."

Great. So I'd better be better. "Got to earn back trust."

He nodded. "Ice time is never a given."

I rubbed the heel of my hand into my forehead. "I should know that."

The Swedish kid was sitting to the other side of me. "Lots of change." He gestured to his head. "Scrambles you up, yeah?"

I croaked out a bitter laugh. "Yeah." Then I sheepishly added, "We met in camp, but I don't remember your name."

That got me a hint of a smile from the blond-haired forward. "Alfie Joelsson."

"Jolly," Jon cut in. "We call him Jolly Green Giant."

Alfie threw a towel at Jon. "You do not!"

Another laugh came out of me, one not quite as bitter. "What do you want me to call you?"

Alfie nodded. "Al is fine. That's actually what they call me on the ice."

"Jolly," Jon said, in a sing-song tone. "Green Giant."

"Al it is," I replied. That got me another soft smile from Alfie.

It felt good to connect to someone on the team. I glanced over at Jon, who was still beaming. Two someones. Desire—treacherous desire—tugged at me whenever I spent too long looking at Jon. He was something else, really. Beautiful, with his pale skin and dark hair that couldn't decide if it wanted to be black or brown. And those brown eyes that danced when he smiled. Alfie said something in—Swedish,

I guess. To my surprise, Jon quipped back in the same language.

Jon had no accent. Or rather, he had a pretty typical North American hockey accent. Probably spent some time in Canada, but how he spoke was more US-oriented. The point being, he didn't have the accent Alfie had. At least when speaking English. But whatever he'd said to Alfie came out as if he'd been speaking Swedish his whole life.

But there was no time to ask him about that, even if I had any idea how to broach "Hey, you speak another language?" without seeming like a complete jerk. I was already pretty far into that territory as it was, and we were getting ready to get back onto the ice.

I'd love to say that my game somehow miraculously improved, but all the shit that had gotten me here was still there. All my shots on net went wide. I even had a beautiful look at a big old gaping hole the goalie had left for me and couldn't get the fucking puck into the net. For fuck's sake, a five-year-old could've, but I flubbed the shot, and it flew right over the crossbar.

My passes weren't crisp, which led to a couple odd-man rushes, and I collected two penalties, a high-stick in the second period and tripping in the third. Luckily, both times, the Otters got the kill. And the Otters got goals, despite my shit play. Both Alfie and Jon collected assists, and I tried to memorize the names of the goal scorers. Especially since Coach had pretty much nailed me to the bench in the third after I returned from the penalty box.

I was still a fuckup, wow. No wonder no NAPH team had wanted me. Maybe those two years before this one had been a fluke, just like social media and some reporters speculated. Luck, not actual skill.

Unwanted.

At the end of the game, I went out for fist bumps and to thank the goalie, then headed into the room. There was enough chatter and good spirits (and oh God, was Jon loud and happy and perfect, all sweaty and bubbly) that I could get out of my gear, slip off to shower, dress, and get the hell out of there. There was a post-game meal in the team lounge, which semi-surprised me because I'd heard that a lot of PHL teams didn't do that. I guess the Otters were serious about keeping their players in shape. The Lions owned the Otters, so maybe that had something to do with it, too.

I was in no mood for food, though. Figured I could pick something up on the way back to my hotel. Heck, there was a chain rib place right near the hotel.

God.

I was staying at a hotel on the edge of a strip mall, next to a bunch of big box stores and chain restaurants and playing in the PHL because I was a fuckup. So much so, that I suspected Coach Macintosh would be on the phone to JR soon, and he'd bust me down to the HLENA. I gripped the steering wheel and drove right past the entrance to said strip mall. My head was not in a good place and sometimes driving helped, so I just kept going. GPS would get me back, so I didn't worry about getting lost.

Fifteen minutes later, I was driving down a back road with no idea where I was except that it was dark, late, and I still felt like shit. Then my phone pinged with a text. Fuck. No one texted me this late except my mom. I pulled over into what seemed to be a tiny parking lot next to a commercial building of some kind. It had a *For Sale* sign bolted to it. I picked up my phone.

The text came from an unknown but local number, judging by the area code. There was the message I'd ignored before, the one welcoming me to the team. The new one said:

> Meet me at the bar?

My heart ticked up a beat or three. At that moment, going to Jon's gay biker bar seemed a better plan than driving aimlessly around the hills of Westmoreland County until my head settled. Especially since I wasn't sure it would settle any time soon.

> Okay.

After I texted my response, I pulled up my map app. The bar's address was still in my recent history, so all it took was a tap on the screen, and then a voice was telling me to turn around. Ten minutes later, there was the bar, and my phone told me I'd arrived.

When I entered, I swear every head in the place turned. All those eyes on me, and something told me they all knew who I was. Probably had the night before too.

Shit. Oh God. Maybe I should leave.

"Hey, babyface," Ella called out from the bar. "Grab that booth over there."

I headed over to where she pointed, and took a seat. A moment later, Ella set a glass of water down in front of me.

"Everyone knew who I was, I guess."

"Not everyone," Ella said. "Bunch of folks here aren't into hockey. They know Jon plays, but that's about it. The rest of us? Yeah, we knew."

I cradled my head in my hands. "I'm so fucking stupid."

She snorted. "No more than anyone else, sweetie. You want a beer?"

I did, but not having anything to eat was catching up with me. "Water's fine. Is there—do you serve food?"

"No," came Jon's distinctive voice. "Just nuts and pretzels and snack mix. Running a bar is hard enough without having a kitchen. Didn't want the added complication. But I brought food because I thought you might be hungry. God knows I am." He set down two large paper bags onto the table. "Hi!"

I stared at him, with his bright and cheerful expression and tousled wet hair. He was wearing his scrumptious leather jacket with an Otters hoodie peeking out beneath.

"You want a beer, Jon, or water?"

"Oh, water, please. Thank you, Ella."

"You got it."

Then he was sitting across from me, pulling takeaway boxes out of the paper bags. "I don't know what you like, so I just grabbed some of everything they had tonight."

From the post-game spread, I realized, as he opened the boxes to reveal different items. Salad. Fish. Chicken. Steak. Vegetables. Pasta. Sure, it wasn't the sushi that sometimes appeared after Lions games, but my stomach rumbled loudly enough that Jon's smile widened.

"How..." But it really didn't matter how he knew I hadn't eaten, so I changed my question. "Why are you doing this?"

He stilled and watched me, blinking a few times. His not moving was almost unnatural. Then he settled into the booth a bit more. "A couple reasons. I'm captain and I like to make sure my teammates are in good shape and not doing anything silly, like punishing themselves by not eating."

I flinched. Maybe I had been doing that. I didn't know anymore. I reached for my water glass.

"But also, I like you. I wasn't flirting with you last night just to be an ass, you know."

That had me sputtering, trying not to choke on the water I'd just sipped. "What?"

That smile was coupled with a hint of flush on his cheeks. "I'm not going to lie about it." Then he pushed a few of the paper containers toward me. "Please eat."

That was a redirection if I ever saw one, but I was hungry, so I took up the biodegradable bamboo utensils he also pulled out of the bags, and got to work on some of the pasta with chicken and broccoli and the salad.

Ella brought water for Jon, and then retreated, so it was just the two of us again.

"I'm sorry," I said.

"For what?"

"For being a shitty hockey player." I paused, then added, "And a shitty teammate."

"Ah, well, the latter, thank you for realizing it, but what you did with Alfie went a long way there." He grabbed salad and dropped some steak on it. "For the former, you aren't a shitty hockey player."

I stared at him. "Dude, did you *see* me out there tonight?"

"Absolutely." He took a few bites, then added, "Not your best night, clearly. But I've watched you play. You're good."

I shook my head. "Not anymore." *Useless.*

Jon seemed amused as he watched me, though not in a malicious way. There was warmth to his mirth and a friendliness—or more—that was confirmed by the faint color he still had in his cheeks. He *did* like me. Finally he put down his fork, folded his hands, and asked, "Do you know who my father is?"

His *father*? Why would I know that "No, I—" Wait. He spoke Swedish. His last name was Eriksson. "Holy shit, are you Gunnar Eriksson's kid?" He'd been a Hockey Hall of Fame player, a number-one draft pick, and one of the best centermen to ever play the game. He was also blond and blue eyed. But studying the sharp angles of Jon's face, I could see a resemblance.

Eriksson was a common enough name that I didn't put two and two together. There were three Erikssons in the NAPH alone, and I knew none of those guys were related to the Shifty Swede.

"Yeah, I'm Gunnar's kid. One of them. I have a sister, too. She's a research biologist working on curing cancer." He shrugged, "And I'm an okay PHL hockey player everyone's forgotten about."

Now my cheeks heated, but he waved that away. "No, seriously. How often do you hear about Gunnar Eriksson's kids?"

Never. People still occasionally talked about Eriksson when another Swede got drafted high or had a breakout year as a forward or something like that. "I honestly didn't remember he had kids. I mean, I was eleven when he went into the Hall."

Jon flinched slightly. "I was eighteen," he murmured. He was unusually silent after that, peering out into the bar like he was looking into the past.

His words caught up to me. "You're more than an okay player."

At that, his good humor came back, and he laughed. "No, I'm just okay. My skills are fine, but not NAPH quality. I belong here." He pointed at the table. "*You* do not."

I skewed up my face and looked down. "Maybe I should be in the HLENA instead."

At that, Jon kicked me gently under the table. "Stop that."

"It's true."

"You know it's not," he said. "You're *twenty-two*. Your whole career is ahead of you. Everyone has slumps, Drake. It's how you deal with them that counts."

I shook my head and poked at my salad. "I'm nearly twenty-three, and this doesn't feel like a slump. It's feels like... like... reality." Back to the baseline I should've been at.

"What happened to you?" he asked, so very gently. "You don't have to answer that if you don't want, but something took the wind from your sails." He tapped his head. "Up here."

I flicked another piece of lettuce. "Nothing happened to me. I just ran out of luck, I guess." I ignored the memory of those messages from my sperm donor that I'd snapshotted. The ones I'd not told anyone about.

Jon grunted. "It's not luck." He resumed eating. For a while, that's what we both did, and silence drifted between us, despite the general noise around the bar. The music, the chatter, the clack of pool balls from the back, those faded into this heaviness that seemed to blanket the booth.

Finally, Jon spoke. He didn't look at me, but it certainly felt like his entire attention was on me. "How old were you when you started learning to play?"

The memory was visceral and almost painful, despite how much joy was in it. Or maybe because of that. "Five. I grew up outside of Philly and they had one of those programs where you could try hockey for free. Get some lessons and gear, you know?" I could still smell the rink and hear the echoes of shouts and the blades on ice. "Best day of my life."

A flash of teeth at that. "I don't remember when I wasn't

on the ice. There are videos of my father and me on the practice rink when I was something like eighteen months old." He chuckled. "Everyone thought I would be like him." He gestured around at the bar. "Didn't work out like that. I'm not my father. I can see the game like him, I know what's supposed to happen, but I'm not as physically gifted, so I can't actually do what I need to fast enough. Used to really bother me. Spent a number of years incredibly upset that I was always being bounced between the NAPH and the PHL because I felt like I *had* to live up to my father's legacy."

"What happened?" I had a hard time imagining this man being anything but upbeat. Granted, I hadn't known him that long, but even on the bench when we'd been down two goals, he'd been chattering away at the team, smiling and happy.

Jon got that faraway look again. "I was up in the NAPH, playing for New Jersey, and was having a rough go at it. I missed a stellar pass that would've been the tying goal if I'd had better hands. Faster reactions. I was so angry with myself, so upset that I broke my stick when I came off the ice, and nearly took out the coach with the shrapnel. There were discussions about my anger issues."

I really couldn't imagine him that upset. Didn't fit with the picture of the man before me. "They send you down again?"

"Of course. And traded me not too long after." He chuckled. "I was a mess, to be honest. And it hurt, because I absolutely love hockey. I can't imagine not playing." There was such passion in his voice, and the way he leaned forward as he spoke. "It's all I've ever wanted to do in my life, from the time I realized what hockey was until now.

I've *always* wanted to be a hockey player." He took a breath. "And I almost lost that."

I paused and watched him, and for the first time, I caught a glimpse of sadness in Jon. Then it smoothed over. "After the trade, as I was scrambling to pack my life up, my father showed up."

"How'd he feel—I mean—did he want you to be a hockey player?"

Jon's smile was beautiful. "Papa? God." He shook his head. "Maybe you can meet him someday, because it's hard to explain, but honestly, all he ever wanted for me and Sofia —my sister—was for us to be happy. And that's what he told me. If hockey was making me miserable, I didn't have to keep playing. He didn't need me to be him. I could be anything I wanted—he just wanted happy, healthy kids."

That stopped the breath in my lungs for a second. Because that's all my mom ever wanted for me. And here I was—not happy. With my mind a mess. "But you kept playing."

"Yeah. Like I said, I love this fucking game. I told him I didn't want to embarrass him by playing in the PHL. And he told me that he would never be embarrassed by me. I could play rec league hockey and he would be proud. I could never pick up a hockey stick again, and he'd be proud of me, because I was his child. I was enough, no matter what." Jon's voice broke a little. He cleared his throat, took a sip of his water, then smiled. "So I decided to see if I could be good enough for the PHL and stay pro, and well—" Once more he gestured around him, and beamed. "It's worked out."

I stuffed some more food into my mouth, mostly so I didn't have to speak while I figured out what even to say. Eventually, I took a drink. "So, I should stay—"

Jon shook his head, then tapped the side of it. "I've got the IQ, just not the skills for the NAPH. You've got both. I've seen you play at that level and thrive. Give me a half hour, and I could probably pull up a dozen clips of you playing at an elite level. You've *got* it, Drake. You're actually a dragon out there."

"But your story..."

"Do you love to play?"

I froze. Did I...? No one had actually ever asked me that before. The answer crept over me at first, a faint tingling, then rumbled up, like a wave growing before it crashed onto the shore. "Yes." I almost shouted the word. Then I fell back against the booth's backrest. Because I hadn't loved it tonight. Or even recently. "Shit."

There was that glimpse of sadness. "I don't know what happened between last year and this—and you don't need to tell me—but you need to find that love again, Drake. That passion that makes you get out onto the ice."

"I don't know what happened, either." Not really. I didn't think. I was just... *useless* out there. Like the message from that fucker had said. "I can't score."

He shrugged. "So?"

"Oh my God." I put down my fork and clutched my head. "I don't know if you're helping or fucking me up even more."

He tapped my leg again. "Hey."

I looked up into Jon's gentle, concerned face.

"Tomorrow, get onto the ice, and remember what you love. That's it. Start there."

That—was a good idea, I guess. I let out a breath and lowered my hands, as an absurd question floated through my mind. "Uh... does this count as a date?"

Jon's grin was like the sunrise, then he laughed and that was the best sound in the world.

I GOT TO THE PRACTICE RINK EARLY THE NEXT morning, before any other player arrived. Even before Coach Macintosh. Hank and the other equipment managers were there, though, but they didn't seem too shocked to see a player far before we needed to be at the rink. I grabbed a coffee from the lounge, then started stretching and loosening up.

I'd hated going back to the hotel after the dinner and conversation I'd had with Jon. He hadn't clarified the date comment, but we'd played another game of pool. Jon really wasn't good, so I'd won, but goddamn, that smile—and the knowledge that he *liked* me—well, that had kept me up longer than I'd wanted, once I'd crawled into bed. Alone.

"Teammates can date teammates here?" I'd asked him. I knew the Lions weren't queerphobic, since Brodie Boone's partner, Oliver, was a trans man, but I'd never broached the whole dating your teammate thing there. I knew on some teams, like Seattle, not acting heterosexual has consequences. Seattle had a pretty awful and phobic GM. Hopefully, the league would do something about that jerk someday.

Jon's answer had come easily. "Yeah, as long as it doesn't negatively affect the team." He'd paused after that. "We had that happen once. Guy came through here and slept his way around the team. Wasn't good at all. Bad scene all around. Caused a lot of internal strife, you know?"

"Did you date him?"

Color rose to his cheeks again. "No. I fucked him. A few

times. He was too—" Jon waved his hand. "He had bad vibes, I suppose, and I didn't want any more of that. I don't know how to describe it. Flighty and negatively dramatic, maybe? He was always pitting everyone against everyone. Anyway, after I found out all the shit he pulled with the other guys..." Jon shook his head. "That's why the dates. To get to know someone a little before jumping into bed with them. That whole thing was so soul-sucking."

"Dates, huh?" I'd given him a small smile and he'd dipped his head, color still on his cheeks.

"Yeah, dates," he said, his voice soft and enticing.

Then he'd met my gaze, and the way he looked at me... Jesus. I took that with me all the way back to the hotel and into a shower to rub one out. No idea if Jon was a top or bottom or vers like me. Didn't matter. I wanted that man's lips on me, and him in my bed. Jerking off hadn't done much to settle me down, because my mind was still whirling from everything else *beside* the lust.

I had no idea if what we'd done was a date, but I felt like we were getting to know each other. He cared. He thought I had talent.

Maybe I did. I mean, my goal had always been to make the big show. I'd been told a good portion of my life that I could go that far. I'd made it. Played good for two years, better than everyone, including me, thought I might.

Then I hadn't, and proved at least one person right, I guess.

Maybe Jon was wrong. But he was so sure of my talent, and he was the son of a hall-of-famer.

Then again, he also thought something had happened to me between my first two seasons and now, but nothing had, really. Only that one tense week in the off season when that jackass had messaged me, everything had been normal. And that week? I shook my head. Done and dealt with. Didn't want to think about it, and that had nothing to do with hockey. It barely had anything to do with *me*, other than some random genetics I'd gained from someone who never wanted me at all.

I didn't know why my game was crap right now, why I couldn't score on a completely open net or pucks jumped off my stick seemingly every time I touched one—I did know that it was eating away at me. I tightened up every time I stepped out onto the ice. I'd been trying and trying so hard.

What he'd said, and that memory of being in gear for the first time... I'd wanted to cry. Not out of sorrow or anything, but because of the absolute memory of the moment. How complete and amazing it had been.

Even lying in bed after jacking off to thoughts of Jon kissing and touching me, of me fucking him, those early memories and emotions churned inside. Kept me thinking well after my lust was gone.

Made for a sleepless night, but here I was, stepping out on the ice in gear earlier than most people would. No idea how many times I'd done this between being that little five-year-old and the person I was now. There were no shrieks of children here. My mom wasn't nervously sitting in the stands. It was just me, the sound of my skates cutting the ice, and the slap of my stick against a puck. I took a breath, and there was the cold scent of the ice, the smell of detergent from the practice jersey, and the vague stink of my own gear that no spray ever quite got rid of.

I circled. Stopped and started. Stick-handled. And just —listened. Felt. Let my mind quiet and trusted all those years of practice. I grabbed another puck and launched it at the net. Perfect shot. Went in easily. Nothing I did was very hard or intense, but my eyes were watery and my breath caught in my lungs.

I loved this. I missed *this*. A feeling of completeness, like I belonged out here on the ice. I was lucky this was my job, and... and...

Maybe I *was* good at it, just like Jon had said. When I was out here alone, I could almost taste that truth, like the cold air around me, as if the trace of understanding drifted like the faint smell of ice, concrete, and sweat.

All I had to do was play. Not worry about goals or assists or anything. If I played the game that I loved *with* the love I had for hockey—the goals would come. The playmaking would return. I headed for the bench, grabbed some water from my bottle, then hopped up to sit on the rail and just— stared out at the ice.

Yeah, I could do this. Come back. Swallow my misplaced pride, worry, anxiety and fear and return to the basics. Listen to the coaches. Work hard in every drill. Play with passion. Didn't matter if I was in the PHL, it was still *hockey*.

This game was what I loved. I had to start loving it back and let it go from there.

CHAPTER 4

JON

Drake was already on the ice by the time I got suited up for practice. Mac gave me a pat on the back but otherwise didn't say anything about this turn of events. Like normal, I was geared up and dressed before the rest of my teammates, so I stepped out onto the ice before them.

But not before Drake.

Pretty sure he saw me, but he didn't react at all to my presence. Rather, he continued skating and puck handling, with occasional shots at the net. I went through my warming up routine, stretching out hips and legs and limbering up—all while watching Drake.

His skating was effortless.

I mean, we all were good at skating. You didn't make it to the pro leagues without having decent wheels, but Drake —his skating was just beautiful. The angles, the way he shifted, how fluid his transitions were. The edgework. And the way he stick-handled through it all, as if the puck was magnetically attracted to his blade.

Stunning.

So different from practice yesterday and the game last night.

Without even looking at me, Drake backhanded a pass right to my tape and I stickhandled the puck before sending it back to him. He watched me now, and there was that smile that he'd only hinted at possessing before.

His next pass bounced off my stick, and I had to skate to get it. Not because it was a bad pass or anything—but because I'd been staring at him and hadn't bothered to catch it.

That got me a laugh from him that stopped my breath. I corralled the puck, then passed it back. We did that a few more times before he switched gears, got this glint in his eyes, and came straight at me.

Oh, we were playing this game then, huh? I was reasonably good at stripping pucks away from charging forwards—even if I was one myself—ever since my dad had taught me how.

Reasonably good was no match for Drake, though. He danced around me like I was one of the practice dummies, despite my trying to shove the puck off his stick. I ended up turned all the fuck around, because I could not even hope to keep up with his movements—so I saw him go bar down into the net that was behind me.

"Yo," boomed a loud voice from the gate at the bench, then Clancy was banging his goalie stick against the boards. "Now that's more like it, Dragon! Bring some fire."

Again, Drake laughed, a high and happy sound, and my knees wanted to buckle from the emotions in my soul. Lust —yes. I was very, very human, after all, and he was gorgeous. But also, relief. Because there was the Drake Williams I'd seen when I watched Pittsburgh Lions games.

The rest of the team filed out onto the ice and started

warming up, so I headed to the bench for some water and hopped up to sit on the boards. Mac, in a track suit and jawing on some gum, skated over. "Kid undressed you."

Fucking hell, did I wish that had been literal. I found Drake in the crowd, talking to Alfie. "He's better than me by far."

Mac grunted and watched the players skating. "I'm starting him on the third line. See how he handles that."

"He'll be on the first line before the halfway mark, next game," I said. "You'll see. He'll earn it, too."

Mac smacked my shin with his stick. "Get your lazy ass on the ice, Jonny."

I did as told. A couple minutes later, Mac blew the whistle and started practice.

This time Drake was wholly engaged in every part of practice, working as hard as the rest of us. Listening to the coaches and asking questions both of the coaches and the players. I knew they tried to keep the systems between here and the Lions similar, but there were some differences—we were at different levels, after all.

Drake also engaged with everyone on the ice. Asking for names, apologizing for his shitty attitude yesterday, all that. It went a long, long way to smoothing over the bad taste he'd left in the team's collective mouth.

Bruno Doran—Bruda, one of our alternate captains this season—gently shoulder-checked me. "You know, you're staring at him."

I turned and raised an eyebrow. "So? What's wrong with admiring the flora and fauna of the rink?"

He snorted. "There's already a betting pool going about you and him."

Of course there was. I wasn't the most subtle when it came to my infatuations, and well, I'd already said he'd been at the bar. "Oh good. Maybe Smitty will win this time. With the kid on the way, he could use the extra cash."

Bruda cackled, then sobered. "Smitty thinks he's too young for you."

I turned. "Smitty's calling me old? He's in his *thirties*! I'm not there yet. Not like you."

There was a smile hidden in that brown beard of his. "Tell me that in a month, asshole."

I'd turn thirty in January. A *little* over a month from now. I pushed Bruda away from me. "Drill time, old man."

As I waited for my turn for a penalty-killing drill, I thought about what Bruda had said about Smitty's concern. I knew the age difference between Drake and myself. Seven years. According to his player profile on the NAPH web site, he'd turn twenty-three a few days after Christmas, and my birthday was just after New Year's. A bit of a gap, sure. But not that huge, I didn't think.

We finished up practice, with Mac being pleased with our effort, and reminding us of the road game tomorrow, and when we needed to be here to board the bus. This one, thankfully, wasn't far—couple hours to Harrisburg to play the Pickaxes. It was those trips up to New England or down to South Carolina that *sucked*.

One thing I didn't do was let my eyes wander over the flora and fauna of Drake Williams while in the shower area with the guys. I got myself cleaned efficiently, got dressed and got out of there. I wanted the first time I really saw him naked to be something *he* wanted and asked for.

In the lounge, I grabbed some food and a table. Alfie and Bruda joined me, and before I even had a chance to, Alfie waved Drake over.

"Drake was telling me about this chocolate shop in Pittsburgh that has European candies." Alfie nearly vibrated in his seat. "I think Ebba and I are going to drive in on the off day after the road trip."

Ebba was his girlfriend. They were so stinking *young* and so stinking *cute* together. She was taking classes at the local university, which I utterly admired. "Sweets to the sweet," I said.

"Shakespeare," Drake said.

"Exactly so." *Now* I appreciated the view fully, and met his gaze. "Do you know which play?"

He snorted. "*Hamlet*." His expression turned contemplative, and he grunted, as if his mind had just shuffled something into place.

"Jonny likes to think he's literary." Bruda said. "He really just watches movies."

At that, I rolled my eyes and smiled while I flipped him off. "I can read and speak three languages—well, two and a half. My French is—" I rocked my hand back and forth to indicate so-so. "I'm out of practice. We need a Quebecois player."

"Oh, sure." Bruda waved his fork at me. "I'll tell management to get *right* on that. A French-Canadian player so Jonny can improve his language skills."

There was Drake's stunning smile again. Yeah, that's what I was aiming for. I could stare at that for *hours*.

"You spent time in Montreal, right?" Drake's blue eyes caught mine for a moment before he looked to his food.

"A couple years." Papa started playing there when I was nine, but I didn't discuss my father's career with my teammates. I mean, they knew, of course, but also he was just "Jonny's dad" on the parent-and-mentor road-trip, and he loved that. "But like a lot of things, if you don't use a language, it slips away."

"Some people never had it to begin with," Alfie dead-panned, and looked right at Bruda.

"Hey!" He flicked a pea at Alfie in response.

And that was pretty much how our meal went. Lots of snark, Drake's lovely smile, and me trying not to melt into a pile of goo when he turned those baby blues on me.

I couldn't help notice that he was waiting to leave until I did. On the way out the door, he spoke. "Thank you for last night. I think I needed someone to remind me that I can love hockey."

The air in the parking lot was cold, and the scent of woodsmoke lingered on the breeze. Clouds had made the sky gray, but there was light in Drake, and that warmed my soul. I'd parked next to his SUV, so I leaned against the back of my truck. "If you didn't love it, if I didn't know you loved it, I'd tell you it's okay to stop. But you have a *gift* and love, and there's nothing you can't do with those."

He gaped at me. "You think?"

I nodded. Pretty sure Drake would lift a Cup in a couple years. The Lions weren't quite there yet, but soon. And Drake would be part of that.

His laugh was a puff of smoke into the air. "Feels weird to hear when I'm about to drive back to a hotel room, but—okay. I'll trust you."

"Which hotel are you at, anyway?" There were only so many... and none were exactly the high-end I knew the NAPH teams used.

"The Marriott."

I must have made a face because he raised an eyebrow. "You think it's bad?"

"The hotel? It's fine. The location?" This time, I purposefully twisted my face. "Has the ambiance of a strip mall parking lot." Mostly because it *was* a strip mall parking lot.

He laughed again. "Yeah, but it's that or commute from Pittsburgh, which..." This time he skewed up his face.

That had me blurting out, "I have a guest room at my house. En-suite bath and everything. New players, people coming up or down—I usually offer it, but there wasn't really a good time."

He stared at me.

Words tumbled out of my mouth as the temperature of my face rose. "You can say no. You can always say no to me. You can say yes to the room and no to the..." I waved my hand. "Flirting. I can stop that, if you don't want it. I don't want you uncomfortable, Drake. Just...living in a hotel room... that really kind of sucks."

He cocked his head. "What if I say yes to the room, but want you to keep flirting?"

"Uh." I was kind of surprised steam wasn't curling off me, with how hot I'd suddenly become. I scratched the back of my head. "I can keep flirting. If you want."

God, I hadn't seen that cocky smile before, and coupled with the quirk of his eyebrow—fucking hell. "Do you want to?" he asked. "Keep flirting?"

This man was too much. Or maybe enough. Maybe exactly enough, and that was a scary thought.

"Yes," I said.

He nodded. "Yes to the room. Yes to flirting. And yes to a date."

It was an actual wonder—a small miracle—that I didn't just—self-combust right there. "Uh, are you allergic to cats? Because I have two."

He laughed, and honestly those laughs were the best sound I'd heard all day. "Cats are fine."

I smiled back and gestured to our trucks. "Let's go get your stuff, then."

MY HOUSE WAS A LITTLE WAYS OUTSIDE OF GREENSBURG proper, more or less equal driving distance between the arena and the bar. It was an older home and had a kind of pseudo-rustic look to it, like someone was trying to go for a cabin, but out of brick, and wood and some pine-green paint, I guess. But the inside was spacious and the house was set back from the two-lane road and the neighboring properties to either side were far enough away that I could putter about in the woods, work on my motorcycle, and shoot pucks off my back patio in private.

When Drake got out, he looked quizzically at the house for a moment, then nodded as if to himself. "Is there a stream back there somewhere?"

There was. "How'd you know?"

He gave a shrug. "The trees, I guess. And—" He turned to face me. "I don't know. I can picture you in the woods, sitting on a big rock, watching water."

"Huh." I stared out into the woods. "There's a creek about a ten-minute walk in, and some rock outcroppings to sit on." I turned to him. "Which I do, when I need to think. Sometimes the brain fills up, you know?"

He opened the back of his SUV and pulled out two suitcases. I gestured for him to give me one.

"You're always so upbeat," he said, as he followed me onto the wrap-around porch. "Like a sunny day. I figure you have to have somewhere to go to recharge."

I chuckled and glanced back over my shoulder. "I have lots of somewheres, actually. The woods. The bar. Taking my bike out on nice days. The rink." I unlocked the front door and ushered him inside. "And here."

"You ride a motorcycle?" He stepped in. "Oh—!"

Thor, my orange short-haired cat, trilled and swished his tail. Usually he came and rubbed my legs, but with Drake there, he sat and inspected him.

"Well," Drake said, taking in all of Thor's ginger glory. "He's a handsome—girl? Boy?"

"That's Thor. He's a he." I pointed over to the huge cat tree on the far wall. "Loki's over there."

Loki, my black smoke Maine Coon cat, perched on the tree like the lord of mischief he was.

Drake gawked. "Fuck, that's a big cat."

He was. Twenty-three pounds and three feet of fluff with the look of an absolute gremlin. "Thankfully, he's a sweetheart. For the most part. He can be a little shit when he's in a mood and get into everything, but that's cats for you." Knowing Loki, he'd check Drake out in his own time. "His fur is very soft. But also everywhere."

"Yeah, we had a long-haired cat growing up." Drake looked around beyond the cat. "But that doesn't seem to be that much of a problem right now. This is..." He drank the room in.

One of the things I loved about this house, despite its cabin exterior, was the bright and open interior. You couldn't tell from the front, but there were windows and windows and cathedral ceilings, and airy space in the living room, which led to the kitchen and its panoramic view of the woods that sloped back away from the house.

As for the furnishings, well, Papa once described my decorating choices as biker leather meets Scandinavian sensibility, and I guess that was a pretty decent description.

I kept to lighter colors, mostly, but accented with black leather, chrome, and hints of red.

Drake's pronouncement of all that was, "This seems— very you."

"Come on, I'll show you your room. It's a little less *me* and more IKEA."

That got me the smile I really liked.

We headed to the other part of the house, and climbed up to the second floor. Thor followed. Loki didn't.

Of course, when I opened the guest room door, Thor ran right in, trilling his little head off. "Sorry, he loves these rooms, but I've been keeping the cats out of here, just in case—"

"Oh, that's okay." Drake wheeled his large suitcase off to the side, then crouched. "Come here, buddy. I'll let you hang with me." He held out his hand, and Thor, the loaf that he was, rubbed against Drake's fingers and started purring like a bike engine. "You got the names from the Marvel movies?"

"No, from Norse Eddas." I said, and when confusion swirled in Drake's expression, I added. "Tales. Prose. Poetry. Norse mythology." When Thor rubbed against me, I bent and gave him scritches on the head. "They're like gods, you know? Cats. Or at least *they* think they are."

Drake chuckled, low and soft. "Yeah. I know hockey players like that."

"Don't we all." I thought of Adam, then shook my head. Thankfully, Drake wasn't that way—quite the opposite, in fact. "Let's get the rest of your things, and I'll show you around. House isn't too huge, but there's space."

"Well, it's larger than my place in Pittsburgh *and* you have land." He followed me down and back out to his SUV.

"It'll be good to save some cash. Still have to pay rent there, and now my salary..."

He hefted another large suitcase out of the SUV, and I grabbed a carry-on-sized roller bag.

I winced. "You're still on your ECC... shit." That was a two-way contract. Meaning he got paid a whole lot less here than when he was in the NAPH. "I know a good finance guy if you..."

He shook his head, but there was a small smile on his lips. "First thing Mom had me do when I signed with the Lions was to talk to a sports financial advisor. I'll be fine. It's just..." That smile slipped away. "It kind of sucks. To... well... suck. Then go on waivers and realize no one else wants you because you—"

I cut him off. "You don't suck. You're having a rough patch."

He grunted, and didn't answer until we deposited the last of his things into the guest room—his room, at least for now. "Lions didn't want me, Jon."

God. He looked much as he did before. Beaten down and heaping all of the blame onto himself again.

So I pulled him into a hug. He sucked in a breath, but also relaxed and wrapped his arms around me. "You're wrong. They want you."

"They want the player I was last season."

"You are that player." I felt him inhale to reply, so I hugged him tighter. "Think, Dragon, think. If they didn't want you, they wouldn't have waived you."

He went still, and I pulled back so I could see his face. Those blue eyes were full of emotions. Hurt, disappointment. Confusion. But all of that shifted to something calmer, and then he met my gaze. "They didn't trade me. They could've traded me."

I nodded. "They took a risk, waiving you to send you here, but they did it to *keep* you. Yes, they want that player you were last year and they *know* you're that player. You just need to find your game."

He slid his hands from my body, so I let him go.

"Will you help me?" Those damn blue eyes of his. Still full of worry and hurt, but also a hint of hope.

"Of course." It came out as a whisper.

And that's when Loki sauntered into the room and squawked for attention.

Drake started. "How is a cat that big that quiet, and what was that meow?"

"He's only that quiet when he wants to be. Usually the floorboards rattle when he walks." I stooped to give Loki his due. "And he's a butter muffin. Don't let his size scare you."

Drake squatted down and offered his hand to Loki, who promptly mashed his face into it, and started purring deep and loud.

"Oh shit," Drake said. "He *is* soft. Does he like snuggling?"

I chuckled. "If you leave your door cracked tonight, I can almost guarantee he'll abandon me for you." I mean, who wouldn't want to curl up with this man?

He gave me a curious look, and I answered, "Loki has a habit of claiming anything and anyone I bring into the house."

"I guess someone wants me after all," he murmured to Loki. "But don't abandon your dad, beautiful. I'm sure we can share."

The cats? Yes. I'd share Loki and Thor. But an unusual zing of possessiveness rattled through me when it came to Drake. I had no desire to share him with anyone—at least not in the way I wanted him. "Let's get the rest of your

things, then I can give you a quick tour of the remainder of
the house, and let you settle in."

We unloaded the few items he had left, then I pointed
out the other the rooms on the second floor. "My bedroom."
He peeked in curiously, but didn't comment on the decor—
which was a little less biker and leather, but not entirely
devoid of that, either.

He was much more talkative when I showed him the
next room, which was more or less a library. Complete with
a daybed that was basically a reading nook. "Oh, shit," he
said. "This is nice!"

I wouldn't have necessarily pegged him for a reader—a
lot of pro hockey players aren't, but come to think of it,
being a bookworm somehow fit Drake, too. "It was supposed
to be my office, but then the books took over, so..." I gestured
around. "Sometimes I need somewhere not the rink and not
a computer or game system. I'll come in here and read or
nap or both."

His brows furrowed, as if puzzling out something. "A
sanctuary."

"I suppose." After thinking for a moment, I nodded.
"Yes. That's a good description." Then I added, "Feel free to
borrow anything. Most of it's in English."

He studied a couple of titles. "Yeah, later I'm gonna
haunt this place."

I couldn't help smiling. I wasn't lonely, per se, but the
idea of Drake pursuing my shelves and curling up in that
room filled me with warmth. Especially if I could curl up
there, too.

We did a quick walkthrough of the ground floor, with its
open living room and kitchen, before I showed him the
basement, which housed my home gym and the net where I

practiced my shots. "I have one for the patio, too, for when the weather isn't shit."

"I do want to see that, too," he said. "And it's just cold, not shitty."

True. There was some sun and blue sky in between the clouds. No snow, so everything in the woods was various shades of brown with some greens poking through. We headed out to the patio, and Drake inhaled deeply.

"It smells good out here."

All cold, but damp and earthy with hints of smoke and pine. "I love it. It's so peaceful. Sometimes there are deer by the woods edge. I'd say it's quiet, but there's noise—just nature noise, you know? That kind of quiet. I love people and the bar and the rink, but sometimes, I just need—"

"To be out of your head for a bit?"

I laughed. "I'm never out of my head. I just need quiet sometimes." I paused, then added, "I talk a lot, I know."

"You smile a lot. I like that. You're—you're always happy." He seemed a little consternated by that. "How are you always happy?"

I considered his question, then answered softly, "Well, I've been damn privileged, honestly. I've never wanted for anything. I could live off my dad's money. I *don't*, but it's there and I grew up rich and connected to hockey." I shrugged. "I'm not happy *all* of the time. I have my ups and downs like everyone. Get mad and frustrated, all that. But— I told you the story about my dad wanting me to be happy. That's a good part of it. I'm playing pro hockey. I own a queer biker bar, of all things. I have this." I opened my arms to take in the patio, yard, and woods beyond. "Why shouldn't I be in love with my life?"

He studied me. "In love with your life?"

"Well, yeah." I gestured around me again.

The emotions that swept across his face were innumerable, and the furrows in his brow deepened. "I've never heard—I mean, people say you should love what you do, but...being in love. That's different, isn't it?" He seemed more like he was puzzling his question out rather than asking me. I let the silence sit between us as the breeze rattled a few of the leaves remaining on the trees.

Finally, he shifted. "One's an action, isn't it?"

"Loving is an action. I think 'being in love' is a state *and* an action. Neither are stagnant—both require passion and *doing*. But being is—you exist in that. I guess, I exist in love, and that more often than not, makes me happy."

Drake stared at me.

Fuck. I scratched the back of my head. "I'm shit at explaining this, eh? Why don't you go unpack, and I'll figure out something for dinner."

"Jon." He said my name like one might murmur a prayer, and I felt the sound deep in my bones.

"Yeah?"

"Thank you. For all of this. For sharing your home and your peace." His eyes were blue gray in this light, and full of emotion.

Couldn't help the smile. "I'm grateful I can." Then I nodded at the door to the house. "Come on. I'll grill some steaks and you can get settled."

There was the smile I'd wanted to see, peeking out from the storm that was Drake. "All right."

Just two words, but that smile and that utterance settled my soul.

CHAPTER 5

DRAKE

I hadn't realized how awful living in a hotel room had been until Loki walked into the room and sat in my suitcase while I was unpacking.

Damn, that cat was huge. When stretched out in the suitcase, he took up one entire side, almost. And this was a full-sized one, not a carry-on. I gave him a pat on the head. "I'm gonna need to get the rest of that stuff out, buddy."

He pushed his head against my hand and started to purr, which sounded kind of like a motorcycle engine.

So I moved on to one of my other suitcases.

I hadn't brought *that* much with me. Suits. Some casual wear. T-shirts and shorts. I wondered what Jon wore around his house. I'd seen him in a suit and in chaps and a leather jacket, and in Otters team sweats. Also half naked in the locker room. Those tattoos of his were something else.

Loki took an interest in everything I touched, and fuck, he was... long and massive and loudly purring at me.

"I guess you really are marking me as yours, huh?" This smoky dark lion of a cat. Felt weirdly odd to be part of something in Jon's life other than hockey.

His giant cat liked me. Life couldn't be that bad, could it?

Eventually, despite Loki's help, I got all my clothes put away in the huge closet, my toiletries unpacked into the bathroom, and my few books, tablet, and laptop set down on the desk. One of the windows in the room looked out toward the side of the house. I could see both the road and the edge of the woods behind, depending on which why I stared.

This place was kind of amazing. So different from my apartment in downtown Pittsburgh, though I loved that space, too. I felt—liminal. I think that was the word... caught between two times and spaces. I was an NAPH player playing in the PHL and I felt like a failure, but also I had so much of my career ahead of me. I wanted to tell Jon about my life, what was rattling around in my head, but I didn't even know where to begin. He'd shared an awful lot of himself with me in the past—God, had it only been two days? And this place, this peace, stress and worry peeled off me just being here. But what was left was—a hollowness. I'd been fine on the ice this morning, but now?

I didn't know what I was now. Liminal. Between.

Fuck. I picked up my phone and scrolled through my contact list until I got to the sports therapist I'd had sessions with my first season. Put my phone back down. Sat on the bed and pet Loki, who crawled into my lap.

And that's where Jon found me when he climbed the stairs from the ground floor and appeared at the open door.

"I see Loki has decided you're his now." Jon's smile was magnificent. "The little traitor."

"There is nothing little about this beast." I scratched under Loki's chin. "You're a big, beautiful monster, aren't you?" I crooned at him.

Loki closed his eyes and, remarkably, purred louder.

Jon chuckled. "He likes you a lot. He's friendly with everyone, but your lap is the first one he's ever gotten in on day one." He shifted his gaze around the room. "You settled in?"

"Yeah, as much as I can. This is so much better than a hotel."

"I know, right?" he said.

When he wasn't smiling, Jon looked like one of those sly foxes, like a trickster deity. But smiling like that? He was—I don't know—a prince. Something out of a storybook. Perfect. Beautiful.

Yeah, I'd been swept off my feet. He hadn't even kissed me yet. What the hell would it be like when he did?

I ducked my head. "Thanks again. I know you said you do this a lot, but I was... I was shitty coming in here and you didn't..."

"Drake."

I met his gaze. His smile was softer. "It's all good. Turn the page." He nodded in the direction of the steps down-stairs. "Come down and eat."

I followed him down to the dining area off his kitchen. Jon filled the silence, as he sometimes did. "I forgot to ask you how you like your steak, so I did one medium and one medium rare and you can have either." He leveled me with a look. "If you want it more done than that, tough. I'm not burning it for you."

I laughed outright at that. "I usually order medium rare, but I'm fine with either."

He indicated the seat I should take, so I sat. Along with the steak, there was also a heaping amount of salad, and some kind of mixed grain and vegetable dish, plus a bottle of red wine. All of it looked good.

"You cook often?" A lot of the guys in Pittsburgh got meal services, even the guys with partners. I understood, really. We eat a lot, have particular dietary needs, and fuck if I wanted to cook that much. Plus, many of the guys have kids and given our travel schedule—well. I didn't envy their partners having to run a household by themselves a good portion of the year.

He shrugged in a way I was taking to mean 'yes but I'm going to downplay it.' "I like to cook," he said. "Honestly, though, it's so much easier to cook for two than one, so I'm grateful for the company."

That look... yeah, that was interest, though it was pretty obvious he was trying to downplay that, too. While we ate, I fished around for something to say, and skittered over everything that had been churning around in my head all day. "You talk about your dad a lot... what about your mom?"

His eyebrows rose, though not in any defensive way. "Oh, well, most people know my dad and of course he had a huge impact on me skating in the first place, then all the noise about me... but Mom... Mom is..." He seemed to search around for words. "She's so strong. Put up with a lot from the media because she wasn't a typical hockey wife. Had her own career. Kept her own career. Hell, kept her name. But like Papa, maybe more than Papa, she wanted us happy and fulfilled in whatever way we chose." He paused. "She cried the day I got my first NAPH goal. She also encouraged me to buy the bar when I told her I was thinking about it. Helped me with the financial planning and all that. Thought it was a good investment and also good for the community. It's a little conservative out here, so she thought having a safe space for queer people was important, for both me and others." He gave another one of those shrugs.

"It was only my mom and me," I said. "She's the only one on my birth certificate. Got pregnant in college with a hookup, and the dude wanted nothing to do with her or a kid. When she chose to continue the pregnancy, he signed over all his rights, then vanished." Which was ironic, I thought, given those DMs I'd gotten. I pushed some of the salad around. "But it was good, growing up. Hard—we didn't have huge amounts of things. She was an accountant, and her firm was really flexible, so when I wanted to keep playing hockey, she made it work."

Jon somehow knew when not to fill silences, too. We both ate a little more before I added, "I think that's why I sometimes think it's a fluke I even made it to the NAPH. I'm not typical. I had a lot of used or hand-me-down gear as a kid. We could only donate so much to the teams... all that."

He made a sour face. "That's one of the things I wish were different. Hockey's expensive. It's hard on kids who are disadvantaged or minorities." He met my gaze. "Sorry you ran into that."

"I mean, there are more and more programs to try hockey for free. Scholarships. All that. I was better off than some other kids, so I shouldn't complain that much. But—I guess it sank into me. And this season..." I shook my head. "My rookie season was unexpected. Everyone, including me, thought I'd slow down the next season."

"But you didn't."

I'd scored fifteen goals my rookie season. Twenty the next. "No. And this year, everyone thought I could score thirty, you know? Get fifty points. But obviously..." I gestured dismissively. "I had, what, five points and a single goal? Then they waived me. Then no one claimed me."

There was that sour face again. "Being claimed or not is

about timing and cap and roster space. Really good players pass through all the time."

"Yeah, I know that. Except I don't, you know?" I shook my head. "I guess— When I first joined the Lions, the team put me in touch with a sports psychologist. It helped the transition. I keep thinking I should call her, I guess."

He gave a small nod, then added with a gentle voice, "It might help. Don't think it'll hurt." His cheeks ruddied, and he looked down at his plate. "I studied sports psychology a bit, when I became captain, because I didn't want to screw people up and I figured it might help." He nodded again. "Yeah, that's a good idea, to call her."

"'Cause I'm messed up in the head?" I tried to sound playful.

He huffed a laugh. "We're all messed up in the head, Dragon."

I don't know why hearing him use his nickname for me warmed my heart so damn much, but I couldn't help smiling back at him. "I guess."

He got that fox look again. "Want to cheat and have dessert?"

I laughed. "Sure. Can I clear the table?"

We both got moving. Dessert, it turned out, were these brownie bars with raspberries and chocolate chips. Rich, but not as sweet as I'd expected. "Don't tell me you bake."

"I don't bake," Jon replied. "I leave baking to the pros. I stalk bakeries and figure out their best treats, then I give them money."

"See, that's the way to do it." I raised my wineglass in a mock toast.

After we'd finished everything, I helped Jon clean up. "How'd you get into riding?" I gestured toward a ceramic jar he had in the shape of a motorcycle.

"Tried it once and loved the freedom of it. Reminded me a lot of hockey, strangely. I think that was the only time Papa ever grilled me about anything I'd done... buying a bike. I mean, I had to get a license to ride and all that. I took some classes at a local community college. And I'm as careful as I can be."

But it was still a dangerous pastime. This time, I was the one to give him room to continue.

"I don't ride in bad weather. Avoid highways. All that. Red Dog scoffs at me sometimes for that, but he's a far better biker. I know my limitations. I still love it, though."

I didn't ask who Red Dog was. I suspected he was someone from the bar. "Yeah, that's what keeps me from thinking about it. Just—I wouldn't trust myself. At least with a car or truck, something bad happens and there's airbags and stuff."

"Exactly," Jon said. "It's fun, but it's absolutely okay to be that person who only goes out on a nice day and sticks to familiar roads, you know?"

"Well, you do look hot in the leathers."

That got me a smile that set my heart racing. "I know."

Well, fuck. Suddenly, I was very warm and I was sure my sweats weren't hiding my interest at all. "Was that a date?" I flailed my hand at the dining table.

That got me a cackle. "Do you want it to be?" Before I could answer, Jon turned his three thousand lumen smile down to something less blinding. "It's been an eventful day, and we have a couple hour bus ride to Harrisburg tomorrow. Let's come back to that later."

Probably the best plan. I wanted Jon. A whole lot. He was—well, basically a walking wet dream. He was also nice, and sweet. And the captain of the team I was on. Still... "I want that dinner date," I murmured.

His answer was equally soft. "So do I."

When I met his gaze, I saw the same desire I felt smoldering there and attraction crackled between us.

It was only a matter of time—the right time. Which wasn't now, given everything I'd talked about with him tonight.

But I had no doubt, we'd get to those dates pretty soon.

I GUESS I SHOULDN'T HAVE BEEN SURPRISED WHEN Kara, the psychologist I'd worked with before, texted me back pretty quickly. Nor that she set up an online appointment for the next morning before I had to head in for practice. I almost felt silly as I sat there waiting in the "lobby" of the connection. I felt a ton better today—probably because I'd slept like a rock the night before. It was so quiet at Jon's. Loki had curled up near me and purred while I'd nodded off. He must have wandered back to his dad at some point, because he wasn't with me when I'd woken. Now, I'd shut the door completely and waited for Kara to join.

When she did, I noted her hair had gotten longer, but she still had that shrewd look and that comforting background in her office. "Hi, Drake. How are you doing?"

"Fine," I said, automatically, then huffed at myself. "Well, not that fine, I guess."

"Uh huh. What's going on?"

I spent the next several minutes blathering it all out. The shitty start to my season. Getting sent through waivers and not being claimed. All the stuff that I'd hinted at with Jon came tumbling out. Hell, I even told her about Jon and the bar and discovering he was captain and how stupid I felt because I should've known who he was.

"And now you're living at his house."

My face heated. "Yeah, but he's not pressuring me or anything."

Kara nodded. "In fact, from what you've said, he's deliberately holding back, but not out of rejection."

"No, I know. He's... really just... thoughtful, I guess. Kind. I mean, I haven't dated a lot of people, but mostly they've been concerned about themselves. It's like Jon takes me into consideration."

"Partners should," she said.

Partners. That word rattled around in my brain, and I shook it away. "But that's my love life—or what might be my love life. I need help with the hockey part of things."

"Okay. Let's talk about that."

We did, but it was all the same stuff I'd told her before, though I added in the conversation with Jon about loving hockey and trying to find that again. "I guess I just want to prove that I can still play."

"Prove to who? Jon? Yourself? The Lions?"

That dirtbag, my brain supplied. "Oh, shit," I said.

I'd screen-capped the direct messages on my Instagram account before I blocked the fucker, just in case. *You're probably just like that bitch. She wasn't good for anything either. It's amazing you even exist.*

"Drake?"

"Uh. So I got some weird messages this summer, from a guy claiming to be my father."

Kara paused, obviously taking in the information I'd just chucked at her out of the blue. I wondered if I'd looked like that the first time I'd read jerkface's first message. "Go on," she said.

"At first, I thought it was someone trying to defraud me

or something, but the guy's name was correct, and Mom's the only other person who knows his name."

Kara paged back through her notes, probably trying to remember my family situation. It'd been a while since we'd talked, so I filled her in, giving her close to the same recounting I'd given Jon. "I'm positive it was him." I paused. "He wanted money. A bunch of money. Said I owed him, since he was my 'dad.'" I air-quoted the last word. "I told him, very politely, that he gave up all rights to me, my mother raised me, and I have no obligation to him because he donated a little bit of genetic material to me. He said some pretty shitty stuff after that." I filled her in on how I'd handled the situation.

"Did you tell your mother?"

"God, no. She doesn't need that shit. You're the only one I've told."

She stared at me. "You've been carrying this around for months, alone?"

"I mean..." I shrugged, though that itchy feeling in my brain started creeping up, "It's not a big deal?"

"Do you believe that?" She cocked her head. "Because it sure sounds like it's a big deal and you've bottled it up, to me."

The itching headed down my back. "I guess it *is* affecting me. Because I bet he's *loving* the fact that I've been playing like crap and got sent down to the minors." I shook my head. "It shouldn't affect me.

"But you want to prove to him that you can still play hockey at an elite level?"

I ran my hands through my hair. "Maybe?" I squeezed the word out. "I don't know. It's stupid."

She gave me a comforting smile. "It's not stupid, it's human." She paused. "You were hit with a pretty heavy emotional burden unexpectedly. That's enough to throw anyone off their game, both metaphorically, and in your case, actually."

I gripped my head. "Ugh. Okay. Maybe." I looked up. "So how do I get through it?"

"Let me offer you some suggestions for overcoming that train of thought."

Together we worked through some tools and coping mechanisms. Stuff I already knew, but kind of fell out of using when I was doing so well. Then we set up a time to follow up, and we ended the session.

I rubbed my face. That had been exhausting, and I still had a practice, a bus ride, and a game ahead of me. When I wandered downstairs, both cats and Jon were in the kitchen. The cats were swatting at each other on their cat tree—with Thor taking the higher ground over his monster of a brother, though Loki trilled when he saw me, and trotted over.

Jon, sitting at the island on a stool, smiled over his coffee cup. "He really does like you."

I gave Loki a pet on the head. "I guess so." Loki rubbed up against my legs and followed me when I went to give Thor a pet, too. "I talked to my therapist this morning," I said while focusing on the cats.

"Oh? How'd that go?"

I rolled my shoulders. "Hard. We dredged up some shit I didn't want to deal with, and now I have to." I finally met his gaze. "You were right. Something did happen."

His eyebrows lifted. "Would you like some coffee?"

"Oh my God, yes." I was dying for a cup.

He rose. "How strong? Do you want anything in it?"

"Strong, and no. Black is fine."

He whipped up something using some complicated-looking coffee machine and presented me with a cup that smelled like it might revive the dead. It was absolutely perfect, and I groaned appreciatively.

When I sat next to him at the island, he bumped my shoulder. "Do you want to talk about it? You can stay no, but sometimes sharing the burden helps a little? I'm sure you have things worked out with your therapist though."

Was that...nervousness I sensed between that tumble of words? I took a sip of coffee and thought about what he asked. "I...want to talk about it. But when do we have to be at practice?"

He flipped over his phone, which had been laying screen down, and there was a photo of Loki and Thor as his lock screen and the time in big, bold numerals: 9:03.

Maybe enough time. We didn't have to be on the ice until eleven. I spewed out a version similar to what I'd told Kara.

When I'd finished, Jon gave my arm a gentle squeeze. "That's a lot.

"That's what Kara said." I sighed and sipped my coffee. "I did let it get to me, but the thing is, I'm most angry about what he called my mom, and I don't want to tell her it happened, but I guess I have to? She doesn't need that old shit dredged up."

Jon grunted, then drank a mouthful of his coffee. His brows creased, then smoothed, and he met my gaze. "Your mom is strong, and I bet she wouldn't want you to carry all of this by yourself. I think you should tell her." He toyed with his cup. "Obviously, she's not useless! She raised you! Has a good career, from what you said. She probably won't be surprised by anything that asshole said, just mad he said it to you."

That was all true. Maybe I could call Mom and tell her. I glanced at the time on Jon's phone, then finished my coffee. "We should get ready to go." I'd already laid out my suit, so it was just a matter of cleaning myself up and putting it on. When I made to rise, Jon caught my hand.

"Hey," he said, those dark eyes of his full of emotion. "You're not useless, either. And you're wanted. We want you."

The Otters. I could almost believe that. "What about you?"

God, that smile and that laugh. "What do you think?" He gave my hand a squeeze. "Go put your suit on, Dragon."

CHAPTER 6

JON

It was a good thing I knew these roads so well, because Drake in that suit was completely distracting, enough so that I had to force myself to focus on the roadway, rather than snatch glances of him. It was bad enough that I'd fumbled and dropped my keys when he'd walked down the stairs looking like that. I'd always found him attractive, and certainly had appreciated his appearance when he'd walked into Hideaway, but this morning the good looks had been on another level.

Maybe it was the weight that had been lifted off his shoulders from the morning's conversations, or the quality of the light streaming in from the living room. All I knew was that his curling blond hair matched the bright gold of his tie and pocket square, and the blue of his suit only enhanced the color of his eyes. Stunning. Beautiful. Mesmerizing.

And yeah, I snatched a glance or two while I was driving. Drake was—relaxed. Peaceful. Maybe even content.

"God," he said, "I haven't road-tripped to a game in an

actual bus for so long. Glad it's not one of those sixteen-hour road trips."

"Thankfully, we only have a few that are more than eight. Most are like today—less than five. And we fly sometimes—especially during the playoffs." Not that Drake would be here for those. Hell, I didn't know if he'd be here through Christmas or New Year's.

"I don't mind. I didn't mind back then." Drake shifted in his seat. "You were right—about loving hockey. I used to love those trips. Being with my buddies. Bonding on the road. Playing in different arenas." I heard the smile in his voice as he added, "Beating the crap out of those teams and shutting up their fans."

"Oh, that part is always fun, isn't it? The way the arena goes silent when you increase a lead, or the other team kills a penalty and you score anyway." Those had been goose bump moments in both my career, and while watching Papa win his Cups. "We usually do well against the Pickaxes. We're their curse team, I guess."

That got me a bright laugh as we pulled into the players' lot at the Otters' practice rink. Once we were parked, I was able to turn my attention fully to Drake. "It'll be fun tonight, I promise."

How could someone go so fully from being the personification of a rainy, cloudy day to one full of light? But that was how Drake looked now. "I'm looking forward to it," he said.

We got out and headed into the arena. The team's social media person, Monica, was out with her camera taking photos as we walked in, and I hoped that Drake's photo made it out onto one of the channels today, because asking her for a copy would be embarrassing.

I still might do that, though, because goddamn.

I wasn't the only one who thought he looked good, given the whistles when we entered the rink.

"Dragon's giving Jonny a run for the fancy pants award," Hardy said.

A flush of red touched Drake's cheeks. "Dragon *is* better than Duck," he murmured.

I just chuckled, feeling pleased as punch for that blush, that little smile, and the sunshine that had chased away Drake's clouds.

On the ice, Drake was a new player—or rather, he was the player he'd been up with the Lions for two seasons. Controlled. Fast. Skilled. His wrist shot was deceptive and wicked and his skating sublime.

Mac pulled me aside when I came in from the ice. "I don't know what you did, but that kid's skating like someone cut a weight from his neck."

"He did that himself," I said. But a part of me worried—telling his therapist about the appearance of his sperm donor and sharing that with me must have lightened his spirit. But the psychological weight of that was still there. Yes, he was handling it now, rather than bottling it up, but these types of shakeups had their highs and lows.

Hopefully, Drake had the tools to deal with the lows. Maybe playing good hockey again would help that.

We were back in our suits for the bus ride to the game in Harrisburg. Drake set the suit jacket and tie aside. A lot of guys, including me, did that. They'd get put on when we got close to the Pickaxes's arena.

Drake caught up to me as we were milling around, waiting for the bus to pull up. "Hey," he said. "Where's the best place for me to sit? I know teams have their spots on the bus and plane and all that... I don't want to cause any more problems."

"A couple of the guys move around a lot, so there's not exactly a whole reserved space thing with the team. I mean, except with Clancy and Ivan, but they're goalies, so they're weird."

Ivan cuffed me gently on the back of the head, and said in beautiful Russian-accented English, "I heard that, Mr. Biker Leather Daddy."

God. Embarrassment rose like heat from a July parking lot. "I'm *not* a leather daddy."

Drake raised his eyebrows. "I've seen you in leather."

And didn't that get the boys oohing and ahhing. I rolled my eyes. "A leather jacket and chaps doesn't make you a leather daddy. I'd just rather not lose skin if I bite the road, that's all."

There was more chatter and ribbing, but that ended when the bus pulled up and we helped the equipment guys load our gear.

"So," Drake said, "sit anywhere?"

"Sit with me," I replied. "Unless you hate the window. I sit in the aisle, usually alone. Hate the window."

His lips quirked into a smile. "I love the window."

Good. Very good. I grinned back. "It's all yours, then."

Settling in next to Drake felt normal and right. Alfie eyed me as he boarded, but shook his head and smiled. Bruda punched me on the shoulder. "Do we have to collect yet?"

"I have no idea what you're talking about, but no," I answered. He cackled and moved on.

"What was that?" Drake asked, poking his thumb toward the back of the bus.

I shook my head. "Bets. Whether you and I will hook up. It's a thing that happens. Not just with me, but when-ever anyone is obviously interested in someone. Or when someone starts dating someone, there's sometimes a pool for how long it'll take until they get engaged, that kind of thing."

"Oh." I looked over, and Drake had this amused expression on his face, and he flicked his gaze over my body, and shit did that send a bolt of lust through me. "But we haven't even been on a date yet." He paused, and that smile of his widened. "Right?"

God. I didn't usually get flustered, but I was deep into it now. "Right," I stammered out. Damn me for running my mouth that first night. And damn Drake's mouth now, because I wanted to kiss those lips. This was going to be a long bus ride.

But as the bus lurched forward and we got onto the turnpike, the rowdy crowd that was the Otters settled down. Conversations fell to murmurs under the rumble of wheels over road, and some of the guys settled in for a nap. I'd usually nod off myself, but my mind was whirling through what I'd learned today and wondering what I could possibly do to help Drake out, besides just...listen.

Then again, maybe all I had to do was listen. Still, a thought popped into my head. It was absurd, maybe even irreverent, given the circumstances. Of course I opened my mouth. "Hey, I have an idea of how you can score a goal tonight."

Drake started at my voice, and turned from the window, where he'd been watching the scenery—such as it was— speed past. Apprehension flitted across his face, and I regretted disturbing him. Too late now, so I plowed ahead. "You know those giant cutouts of heads people bring to games?"

His brow creased. "Yeah?"

"So, imagine one of those behind the Pickaxes's goalie,

only it's that asshole. And then hit him with pucks. Repeatedly"

Drake stared at me, unmoving but for the little bumps and shudders of the bus, then the consternation morphed into confusion, exasperation, and then he started laughing. "Oh my God, you're weird."

"I am not. I mean, I am, but not like that. I'm just saying —a little visualization could go a long way!"

"Yeah." That lovely smile shaped his mouth into something truly delightful. "It could." He slipped his fingers into mine and squeezed. "Thank you. For thinking about me."

"I—" My brain caught up enough to stop the words from flowing out. *I always think about you.* "You're welcome." His fingers were warm and heavy in my hand. The connection felt like a live wire, like electricity sizzled between that touch.

His smile softened. "Gonna take a nap," he said before leaning back into his seat and closing his eyes. He—didn't let go of my hand. I didn't let go of his. I'd never felt more dizzy and dumbfounded in my life. I didn't get this way over *anyone*, let alone someone I'd known for a handful of days.

A few breaths had me closing my eyes as well.

Mom used to talk about how she knew my father was the one the moment he said hello to her at a charity event. She'd been the event planner, dressed in boring black slacks and button-down, as she put it, but she said something passed between them in that moment, and hours later, once the event was done, he'd asked her for her number. And that was that.

And this was—this. Terrifying. Exhilarating. Unexpected.

The only thing I could do was hang on and see where this led us.

For this game, I was in my usual spot on the left wing of the first line, with Bruda centering me and Alfie. Despite having played most of his life on the bigger Olympic-sized rinks, Alfie'd taken to the faster-paced game over here in North America and was one of our fastest players. Great on the forecheck. A sneaky shot. I suspected he'd end up on the Lions next year. Maybe be a black ace, if the Lions made a playoff run.

Mac started Drake on the third line with Smitty and Bike. Another test. See if he could bring the energy needed to mix things up with the Pickaxes, who had the well-earned reputation of being bone-crunchers. Drake was—

Drake was *Drake Williams*. From the moment the puck dropped for the faceoff in the defensive zone, he played like he had the first two seasons of his career. A decisive faceoff win, and the puck came to him during the breakout into the neutral zone, he danced through the defense and evaded the back-check, and probably would've scored, if the Pickaxes's goalie hadn't been a number-two draft pick. As it was, the kid barely made the save, and we were all over them until the goalie managed to cover the puck in the mad scramble around the net.

The look Drake had when I skated past him was one of sheer focus and determination, not anger, not even frustration. His mission was to get a puck behind the goalie. Wasn't going to be easy. Their goalie was *on* tonight. A fucking wall. I was sure Alfie was about to score when the goalie twisted in a way that shouldn't have been possible and snagged the puck out of the air.

We skated back to the bench. "How the fuck...?" Alfie shook his head and banged his stick on the board.

"Hey." Drake patted him on the arm. "It was the right idea. Make him move side to side. Just got to do it more. That was *close*."

"But not in," Alfie said.

Drake nodded. "We'll get him."

I caught Mac watching the exchange, and he caught me watching him. A tiny tick up of his mouth was the only sign he was pleased. A couple shifts later, Drake's line went out once more for another defensive zone faceoff. Drake conferenced with the guys, then got set. Whatever he said—holy shit, it was beautiful. His win. The breakout, the speed and long passing. Bike bearing down on the other team's goalie, then the series of short passes that put him out of position, and the beautiful shot by Drake from one knee that sent the puck into the open net.

I yelled. We all did. Drake led the line for fist bumps. When he settled into his spot on the bench he turned to Bike. "What a pass! Perfect. You're great, man."

This time, Mac actually smiled. A tiny one, but yeah. Drake had certainly turned around from the grumpy, seemingly arrogant player who'd arrived a few days ago.

Unfortunately, the Pickaxes tied it up near the end of the period. "Don't worry, boys," I said. "We can get it back."

"Goalie's rattled," Drake said during intermission, to no one in particular. "We get some chances off the rush, they'll go in."

Nods around the room at that.

Drake was right. Early in the second, when Alfie and I got a chance on a two on one, I faked a shot, passed to Alfie, and he slammed it home. Top shelf. All because the goalie overcommitted to me. Thank God my pass had been on point. It wasn't always.

When I got back to the bench, I ended up next to Drake. "Nice sauce on that pass," he said.

"Luck," I replied.

"No. You knew what you were doing." He said it so mater-of-fact that I nearly believed him. Felt like our role had somehow switched, and he was encouraging me.

Of course, the home team would not go away quietly, so of *course* they scored once more near the end of the period.

"Fuck," I muttered. Goddamned screened shot. Not a thing Ivan could've done about it. "We'll get it back."

During the second intermission, Mac shook up our lines, and suddenly, Drake was with me and Alfie on the top line. No one complained. When we went over the boards to take a faceoff outside the Pickaxes's defensive zone. Drake won it back to our D and, as Drake entered the zone, I saw the play unfolding. The way he and Alfie rotated. The way the puck was passed back to the D then up and I knew exactly where I needed to be, especially since not a single Pickax player was watching me.

It was only a surprise to the home team when I skated to the crease, planted my stick, and tipped Drake's shot past the goalie's pads. A moment later, I was engulfed in a hug from Drake. "Yeah!" he shouted, "Let's fucking go!" The rest of the guys crushed me and patted me on the head, then we skated toward the bench for fist bumps.

The arena went silent, but for the cheers of the smattering of our fans in the stands and our bench.

This time, the Pickaxes didn't score near the end of the period, even when they pulled their goaltender to go after us at six on five. After a broken faceoff, Lou managed to get the puck to Drake and he flung it at the empty net with such precision that it hit dead center, even though he was on our side of our blue line.

Game over. We won four to two. Drake had played like the pro he was. I'd even gotten a goal. Alfie was all smiles and the locker room was a riot, as if we'd made it into the playoffs. The boys were all yelling "Dragon!" and congratulating Drake on his three-point night.

I stood back, taking the time to watch them and him and soak in that smile of his. He was as bright as his blond hair and blue eyes. High summer, that man. Not a cloud in his sky right now. This was what I'd set out to do, put that smile on his face.

Hopefully the confidence would lead to more points and more goals and the continuation of that happiness. Drake wasn't built to be storm-cloud gray all the time. This was so much better.

When I moved to my stall to strip off my gear, his gaze met mine, and he crossed the room to pull me into a hockey bro hug and whispered, "Thank you," into my ear.

"Are you kidding? That was all you." I gripped his shoulder and met his gaze.

Fire there, among the joy. "Not all me. Your visualization helped, too."

Exactly what I wanted.

After we'd all cleaned up and devoured our post-game meal, Mac pulled me aside. "Don't get your heart broken," he said.

That was not at all what I expected to hear. "Me?" was all I could get out with my mind whirling.

Mac snorted. "I see the way you look at him, and I've seen that look before on people."

Uh oh. "I'm not... he's not... we're not..."

"Yeah, you are, Jonny. In deep. Kid's gonna go back up, you know that."

I did. And Pittsburgh was a world away for me, more or

less, despite its closeness. "My heart's fine. And he's fine. And I know they're going to call him up. That's the whole point of this." I waved my hand. "Of me being captain. He's not the first guy they've sent down for us to patch up and give back."

Mac snorted again. "He's the first one you've ever looked at like he's the moon and the sun for your sky."

When the hell had Mac gotten poetic? "It's fine. I'll be okay."

"Mmmhmm. I'm just saying." He nodded toward the exit. "Get on the bus, Jonny."

I rolled my eyes and headed out to join my teammates.

THE RIDE HOME WAS ITS USUAL QUIET SELF. MOST OF the guys fell asleep—a combination of the adrenaline wearing off, how late it was, and the lulling motion of the bus. Normally, I'd have been completely out by now, but the conversation with Mac had me wondering exactly how obvious it was that I was *serious* about Drake. More so than just for a tumble in bed.

It was a longing that I'd never felt before. Mom's story ran through my head again. Papa had also recounted that night, and I closed my eyes to better listen to the deep rumble of Swedish in my memory. He'd known, too, the moment he'd met Mom. She'd had the most beautiful smile he'd ever seen—and she hadn't even been looking at him. But he'd known then that he'd do everything in his power to spend the rest of his life trying to keep her smiling like that.

Oh shit. *I was just like Papa.* Fuck.

Weird thing was, if Drake never made a move, if we

never hooked up, hell, if he wasn't into men—I'd still want that smile on that face.

In the seat next to me, Drake stirred in his sleep, turned a little, then slumped against my shoulder. The contact was warm. Soothing. Perfect. Mac was right. I was in deep. And maybe I would get my heart broken—but maybe not. There were ways not to. Assuming Drake was interested in more than a fling.

And if he wasn't? Well, yeah, my heart might hurt. But I wouldn't have a single regret—that I knew, too.

Perhaps it was Drake's warm body, or just my brain deciding it had run long enough today, but weariness finally overcame me, and I joined the rest of the team in passing out after a well-fought win.

CHAPTER 7

DRAKE

I woke when the bus exited the turnpike—we all did, pretty much—and found myself curled up against Jon. He groaned and stretched but didn't seem disturbed by my presence, even giving me a sleepy smile when I sat up. I checked my watch while blinking away sleep. It was late—a little past one in the morning, and I absolutely wanted more sleep.

Despite being tired, my body remembered these kinds of bus rides from juniors and I enjoyed them. The quiet companionship. The team murmuring around me. But more importantly, for the first time this season, I felt like *me* again. Exhausted, yes, but happy with the game I'd played and how I'd skated. I'd scored two goals and helped my hockey team. What was better than that?

I owed Jon a lot. From his first talk with me to opening his home. He was a good captain and a good player. Some-day, he'd probably make a great coach, given that he knew the game really well—that high hockey IQ of his. He was such a kind person, too.

He was also really fucking hot. Even as rumpled as he

now was, those warm brown eyes and wide smile tumbled everything inside my chest.

He patted my thigh. "We're almost back to the rink. Then we'll get you home and to bed."

My brain was a haze of sleepy and horny, so I nodded rather than blurt out something inappropriate. It was *his* bed I wanted to crawl into, but boy, was *that* presuming too much. Jon had been flirty, sure, and yes he wanted more, but we'd yet to be on the date he wanted as a feeling-out process. Despite all of our close proximity, we'd *just* met. He didn't want a meaningless hookup, and I didn't want to *be* a meaningless hookup to Jon.

Once we got back to the practice arena, we got our bags and headed to his truck. "You good to drive?" I asked.

"Oh yeah. I've done this a lot. I mean, I'm tired, but I know the way home, and it's only about fifteen minutes. This time of night, all I have to worry about are critters on the road."

I don't think I'd ever get over how bright his smile was. The air was cold—below freezing—and so was his truck until the heaters kicked in. The cold chased away some of my lethargy, but silence crowded the cabin, and I didn't know how to break it when Jon didn't fill it with his usual chatter.

Was that good? Bad? Fuck. He must've noticed me shifting in my seat, because when we pulled into the driveway of his house, Jon patted me on the knee as if to reassure me. "Hey. We're here."

I knew that. I also knew I wanted more of his hands on me. "Yeah," I said. "It was a good night." Ugh, what a boring thing to say.

He chuckled as we climbed out of the truck, and I wished I had his ability to be that relaxed and at ease.

Content. Truly happy. Just be who I was. I'd only ever found that in moments on the ice.

In the foyer of the house, Jon threw his keys into a bowl on a table by the door, and instantly Thor and Loki were there, meowing their heads off.

"Hi guys," Jon said. "I know, I know. I was gone forever." He rolled his eyes. "Need to feed these guys or they'll never leave us alone."

"I thought you free-fed?" I'd seen the bowls out in the kitchen, and they always had kibble in them.

"Yeah, well, they don't always understand that they can just go eat what's there. Or maybe the bottom of the bowl is showing, so it *must* be empty and they'll starve to death or the bowls are in the wrong place or some random reason." He laughed. "Cats."

It'd been a while since I'd had one as a pet, but I got it. They could be particular beasts. I trailed Jon to see which it was. Loki and Thor circled us like little furry sharks.

Well, one little furry shark and one huge lumbering one that had a permanent peeved look.

"You bozos," Jon said with all the affection in the world. Then he shook the cat dishes. "Okay, they're a *little* low, but you guys weren't going to die." He set about adding food to the bowls.

For a moment, I watched his lean form as he moved around the kitchen. I didn't want to just—say goodnight and climb up the stairs, but staring at him seemed too much, so I hung up my coat in the hall closet and lingered while he finished up.

When he was done, he gave me a sleepy smile. "You need anything? Water? A snack?"

Him. I needed him. I shook my head. "No, I'm good."

"Okay." He put his hands on those hips of his, and

looked around. "I think they're fine here. Let's head up, eh?"

He crossed the living room and toward the stairs.

"Jon."

My touch on his arm halted his steps, and he turned to face me. "Yeah?"

His expression was so open, so gentle. So absolutely beautiful in the dim light of the hallway. "Can I... Can we... Would you..." The words stuck in my throat and the lines of his face morphed toward confusion. "Look, I know we haven't had a chance to go on that date yet, but—can I kiss you? I really need to kiss you."

The lips that I wanted so badly curled up, and he stepped close. Suddenly, it wasn't bewilderment in his eyes, but hunger. I could've sworn a spark lit in his dark eyes. "You can absolutely kiss me," he said, voice low and rough.

We moved together, my hand landing on his shoulder, his cupping my neck, and our lips met. I'd expected something devouring from him, but his kiss was soft, almost sweet. Until I slid my other hand up into that hair of his. Then he groaned deeply and opened to me.

Instinct took over, and before I even thought about it, I had Jon pressed against the nearest wall. His grip around my neck tightened and his other hand landed on my ass. Only need in our kiss now. Tongues tangled and the passion and fire I'd expected from Jon was there. I wanted to slide down his body and worship him on my knees. Especially considering how hard his dick was against me.

Jon broke our kiss and touched his forehead to mine. "Drake." Raspy voice. "You can say no. I need you to know that." He leaned his head back enough for our gazes to meet. "I'm captain," he whispered. "You're staying in my house."

My turn to be confused. "I was the one who asked you for a kiss." And I had him pressed firmly up against the wall of that very same house.

His laugh was a strange nervous bark. "I know. But I'm going to ask you for something, and I want you to know you can say no." He was so damn earnest.

"Believe me, you're not forcing me into anything." I ran my thumb over his cheek. "I can't imagine you forcing anyone into anything, except an opposing player into the boards."

That got me another strangled laugh.. "It's just—I don't want to screw this up."

"Screw what up?"

"This. Whatever *this* is—I want to get it right. And it's late and we're both tired and—"

I stole a quick kiss to stop his rambling. "Jon, what do you *want*?"

He let out a sigh, cupped my face between his hands, and said, "I want you to take me upstairs and fuck me until I can't think." He paused. "I was going to say, 'until I can't think straight', but that's kind of impossible, given that I'm queer and—"

God, this man. I swallowed whatever else he was going to say into a deep, hard kiss, and finally let myself run my hand down his torso to his cock. He groaned again and thrust into my hand.

"I can do that," I whispered against his lips. Then I backed up and nodded toward the stairs. "Your room or mine?"

Jon was uncharacteristically wobbly. "Your choice."

"Yours." If I was fucking this man into a mattress, I wanted it to be the one he regularly slept in. Maybe that was a little possessive of me, but if this were the one time we'd be together, I wanted him to crawl into bed in the coming days remembering my body against his.

I took Jon's hand and led him up to his bedroom.

Once inside, he closed the door. "Cats," he said breathlessly. "Don't need them in here right now."

Made sense. Last thing I wanted was big Loki, or even Thor, jumping up while we were in the middle of things. Or watching us. That would be a little weird.

I gathered him in for a kiss and we began the slow dance of touching and tasting as we stripped clothes off of each other's bodies. I finally got a good view of his tattooed sleeves, which consisted of vines and animals and angels. Some playing cards. Crowns. A flower. I also got a glimpse of the small line of script on his ribs, but I was way too busy with his mouth to read his torso. I'd get there eventually.

I pushed him back against the bed, and he let himself fall backward, legs splaying apart. Taking that as an invitation, I crawled up his body, kissing as I went, until I got to that sharp mouth of his. I didn't think I would ever get tired of him kissing me back. He kissed like he did everything, with passion and purpose and for longer than I thought he might.

When he came up for air, he waved toward the left side of his bed. "There's lube in that nightstand. And condoms... condoms... fuck. They're in the bathroom in a cabinet." He sounded dismayed. "It's probably easier for me to get them than tell you where."

I gave his dick a few pulls and enjoyed the sight of him rolling his eyes back before he squeezed them shut, arched, and moaned.

"Guess you should go get them, huh?" I said.

"You're evil." He didn't sound at all upset, and his mouth ticked to a grin when I let his dick go. "Be right back." He scrambled off the bed and to the bathroom. A moment later, he came back with a box of condoms.

"You don't keep them in your nightstand?"

"Oh, um." He shrugged. "When I have a regular partner, I do. But it's been a while and they kind of reminded me that I really wasn't finding what I wanted with hookups." He sat down on the bed slowly and looked, suddenly, bone-weary exhausted. He gestured between us. "I know this doesn't have that high a chance of being anything permanent, but it... this doesn't feel like a hookup. And I just really want to be with you."

Wow, that was actually pretty heavy, all together. My chest ached for this man. He was so damn happy all the time, but underneath that, how much loneliness lurked? I took the box from his hands, put it on the table with the lube, and then took him into my arms and kissed him. He was pliant and after a moment, folded his arms around me, too.

When I rolled him onto his back, I whispered. "I've wanted you since I walked into your bar. You're so damn good looking. But what caught me was your smile, and how you care about everyone. I don't know what this is either, but it's not a hookup, and I'm going to make damn sure you enjoy every second." I paused and skimmed fingers over his nipple. "And that you can't think when I'm done."

There was that brilliant smile again.

I worked my way down his body, kissing and nipping as I went, pausing over the text on his ribs—which I still couldn't read because it wasn't in English. Swedish, I thought. I nibbled right below that, and Jon gasped, and urged my head lower.

Yeah, okay. I slid my fingers over Jon's hips before I

wrapped a hand around his cock and sucked the head into my mouth.

"Oh my God," Jon moaned. "Fuck, Drake."

Jon was just about the perfect size to suck off. Not too long or wide, and I loved the noises he made, and the way he squirmed and thrust under me as I worked his length into my mouth, and eventually my throat.

I swore he squeaked at that. One high-pitched sound, as if he was completely shocked. When I came up for air, he found my head with his hands. "Drake... Drake, you do that again, I'm gonna come."

I met his gaze, and there was a mix of desire and apprehension there. "You want that? Want to come down my throat then be fucked senseless after you're good and sensitive?"

His eyes widened a bit, and I swear his dick got harder in my hand. "Yeah," he breathed. "God, it's been—" He cut himself off with a laugh. "Yeah. I want that."

I was more than happy to give him what he wanted. I took my time sucking him off, though. Worshiping his dick and edging him with slow licks and sucks and exploration until he was babbling nonsense between begging me to make him come. My name was interspersed with gasps, pleading, and cursing—including something that sounded French and profane. When he was a trembling mess, I finally took him down my throat again. Didn't take much time before he was breathlessly croaking out my name while his cock thickened—then he was spilling himself into my mouth. Jon's moans were deep and glorious, and when I finally came up for air, he was glassy-eyed.

"Holy shit," he whispered. "You're good at that."

"Thanks." I grinned down at him. "It's not all I'm good at in bed."

God, him and his dark hair all mussed up, the sheen of sweat on his chest, and those brown eyes sparkling. He levered himself up, cupped me behind the neck, and kissed me. "Is that so?" he said, when he'd freed my lips.

"It's your lucky night. You get to find out." I paused. "How do you want to—" I gestured to the bed around us.

That got me a chuckle. "On my back, if that's fine with you."

Fucking this man in any way was going to be a pleasure. If all we ever did was me sucking him off, well, that and a few pumps of my own dick would be enough. "Absolutely."

While he grabbed a pillow for his hips, I got the lube and condoms. Sitting back on my heels, I drank in all of Jon. His inked arms and shoulders. His sculpted, lean body with those thick thighs. The devilish look on his face, all angular and foxlike.

This wasn't a man who should ever be lonely. Not with the heart of gold and fast-working mind that went along with that amazing body. "You're so damn perfect." I drew a condom out of the box, and tossed the box back toward the nightstand.

"I absolutely am not," he said. His smile remained. "You know that."

Except he was perfect. And beautiful. And—at least right now—mine.

"Mmmhmm. Whatever you say." I stroked the inside of his thighs and watched his eyes roll back as he sank down onto the mattress. I teased his balls and taint, licked my thumb, then rimmed his hole.

"Fuck," he breathed.

"Sometime, I'm going to eat your ass," I said. "But not tonight."

His reply was a croak.

Watching him like that got me hard enough to put the condom on, then I lubed up my fingers and went back to rimming his hole, dipping a finger in and watching him squirm.

More curses, more pleas, and those imploring eyes as I worked him open and found exactly the right spot. He arched, practically lifting off the bed.

"Fuck, Drake! Please just—fuck me already!"

Well, that was an invitation if I ever heard one. I slicked myself, then eased my way into him. God. The heat. The tightness. I closed my eyes against the pleasure, and we both moaned when our bodies met.

When I peeled my eyes open, Jon was staring up at me, those dark eyes of his intense, his mouth open. I wanted to carve that expression into my brain. Then I started moving, and he gasped.

Fucking Jon was an absolute delight, and though he was on his back, he rocked his hips in time with my strokes until we hit a rhythm that had us both moaning. He was by far the hottest man I'd ever been with, and watching him as I gripped his hips and drove my cock into him was—everything.

He was quieter this time. Less curses, but the moans were long and deep. At one point, he wrapped a hand around my neck to pull us into a frantic kiss, and I nearly lost it. Finally, I breathed his name. "Jon..."

"Can still think," he murmured.

Time to fix that. I pressed him back into the bed, stroked into him until I found the angle that made him lose the ability to breathe without gasping—and pounded him. Relentlessly. Utterly enjoying how he twisted and moaned beneath me and how his hands clenched me and the bed—anything he could reach.

Then his eyes widened. "Fuck—fuck—I'm going to—"

He clenched around me so tight, I could barely move inside him and oh God—I was coming too. "Jon!" My own pleasure crashed like an unexpected wave against me as I spent inside him.

As we came down from our orgasms, Jon shivered in my arms, and I had enough sense of mind to pull up the throw at the bottom of the bed and curl around him. I murmured into his ear, "Can you think?"

All I got back was, "Mmmmph," and he pressed against me. I took that as a no, and simply held him, pleased that I'd managed what he'd asked. We'd have to get cleaned up soon and I needed to ditch the condom, but for the moment, I was content to just lay here.

A moment later, a loud, rhythmic pounding on the door stirred Jon. "Ugh," he said. "That's Loki. He'll do that all night if I don't let him and Thor in."

"So, you'll move for the cats, but not for me?"

Oh, he could think now, because his gaze was wickedly sharp. "I moved quite a bit for you tonight, you know." The smile that followed made my heart flip.

Fuck yeah. The way he'd twisted and writhed and met my thrusts was fresh in my mind. I let out a shudder of a breath, which prompted a gleeful chuckle from him. We climbed off the bed. He headed to the door, and I headed into the bathroom to ditch the condom and clean up.

A moment later, Jon joined me. "I'd suggest a shower, but I'm really fucking tired now and it's..." He looked at his watch-less wrist, then shrugged. "It's really late."

Had to be. I raked a hand through my mess of hair. "I should go bush my teeth." Even as the words left my mouth, his eyes widened in the mirror's reflection and I saw the panic there in the bright lights.

"Please stay," he blurted out. "Of course you don't have to, but if you want you can stay with me tonight. I'd like it, and I think, I think maybe you would, too?"

God, he was always so sincere, so hopeful and beautiful. I desperately wanted to stay. "Yes."

Hope bloomed to joy in him, and I couldn't help drawing him into a kiss. "I still need to brush my teeth, but I'll be back over."

"Good. I'll be here with the cats."

That's not exactly what happened, because Loki followed me back to the other room, sat staring at me while I brushed my teeth and cleaned up more. He gave me a strange little bark as I came out, then led me back to Jon's room.

"Your cat is herding me."

Jon was already under the covers, propped up and reading a book. Thor was curled up at his feet. "Is he? That's strange. He's never done that with anyone before. He really likes you, I guess!"

I snorted. "How many other guys have you hosted at your place and also slept with?"

Oh, the little ruddy spots that lit on his cheeks. "Uh, none, actually. I'm usually a very upstanding captain who never makes a move on teammates I host." He paused. "And I haven't dated anyone in a while. Not since I got Loki, at least, and that's been—" He paused, and seemed to search for an answer on the ceiling. "Five years? Yeah. Five. And he's never herded anyone to my room except me."

"But—" I stopped myself from blurting out the rest, shook my head, then climbed into bed next to him. I went with, "Five's a lot."

Loki lumbered up onto the bed and marched up between us, settled in, and purred, content with the world.

Jon wasn't as content, it seemed. He tucked a bookmark into the pages of his book, then set that aside. "But?"

Yeah, I figured he wouldn't let that slide. I met his gaze. "You're one of the most stunning people I've ever met. And you're nice. Why aren't you married to some... amazing person who'll love and cherish you?"

A whole parade of emotions marched across his face. "Uh. Wow." Then he scratched the back of his head. "Well, first, I think you're overestimating me quite a bit. I mean, I know I'm attractive, but there are tons of better-looking guys out there. I do try to be nice, but I can be crotchety and annoying—ask any of the guys in the room. I can be an absolute pain in the ass." He shook his head. "I've got a pile of flaws." The rapid fire of words fell away. He smoothed his hands over the bed's comforter. "And second—my life is basically hockey and running the bar. Most amazing people want time with you, you know? When it was just hockey—well, the right person never came around, and the bar did, and people needed a safe place so..." He trailed off. "I'm rambling. It's late."

He'd twisted the comforter in his hands. "I did just meet an amazing person." Jon raised his gaze to mine again. "But we haven't been on a date yet, so—"

My heart melted right fucking there. "I've been nothing but a grouchy pain in the ass. Hardly amazing."

That smile of his ticked up. "Well, you weren't exactly a *pain* in my ass tonight..."

Oh my God. I dropped my head into my hand and giggled. "I'm too tired for this." But I beamed at him. "So no date yet, but dating?"

"If you want, yes. I mean—yes. Let's try it?" He paused. "You can change your mind in the morning if you wake up and realize the sex and me aren't that—"

I leaned over Loki, caught the back of Jon's neck, and pulled him into a kiss. When I relented, he was breathy and speechless. "You're amazing. I'm not going to change my mind. We should sleep."

Loki chirped and looked particularly peeved, even for a Maine Coon.

"Sleep," he said. "Probably a good idea."

He turned off the light, and we settled in under the covers, Loki between us.

I shouldn't be in love. This was too soon to be in love. We hadn't known each other all that long. But goddamn, this man. This damn man. He was everything.

CHAPTER 8

JON

I woke to Drake asleep next to me and had to stop myself from giggling like a fool. Felt like I was still dreaming, seeing his mop of curly blond hair and his sweet face pressed into the pillow. I'd have wrapped myself around him, but Loki was stretched out between us, and I wasn't going to argue with a sleepy twenty-three-pound ball of attitude, so I let Drake be.

Sex last night had been... Well, thinking about it curled my toes and had me on the way to a morning wood. Given Drake's deep breathing and my beast of a cat occupying the middle of the bed, another round wouldn't happen for a while, so I sucked in a breath and let my growing arousal subside.

The softness of the light creeping into the room around the edges of the curtains hinted that it was early morning. Well, at least early enough that closing my eyes and falling back to sleep wouldn't be unusual given how late we'd gotten home and—everything after that.

That was not happening. Brain wouldn't shut up.

God, Drake had been perfect. Passionate. Thoughtful.

Gentle at times, forceful and sharp at others. He'd been a fucking tease, but that had been the best thing. I hadn't been kept on edge like that, blown like that, or fucked like that— Actually never. Never like that.

I hadn't bottomed in a while. Hadn't had penetrative sex, either. Mostly quick hand or blowjobs when I felt the itch to let off some steam. Hell, I hadn't even had a BJ or hand job in a long time. Fucking around with Adam had been the last real bit of anything I'd done. Flirting? Yeah. A little kissing and fondling? Fine. My "rules" about dating before sex were more about me giving myself an out than anything else. No one had been worth opening myself up to or for until Drake.

I didn't want to hurt the team. Didn't want to throw my game off. Was busy enough at the bar. I could list a million excuses as to why I hadn't dated anyone in five years, but the reality was that who the hell was going to put up with a queer odd duck aging PHL player who was never going to be more than that? I loved my life, but I knew what it was. It was *mine,* something I'd built from the ruins of everyone else's expectations. I didn't want the burden of living up to anyone's hopes and dreams.

So I just... stopped looking.

Then Drake walked into my bar, my haven, before he'd even walked into the arena we'd share, and I'd been smitten instantly.

I shouldn't have been. But there he was, a man with hopes and dreams that mattered, that could be achieved, and I'd wanted to see that bright star shine again. He'd had absolutely no expectations for me—barely had any for himself other than failure. He'd been vulnerable, and truthful, and here we were, in my bed, after he'd fucked me senseless.

Lovers. Teammates.

At least until he scored in a few more games, and the Lions realized he'd gotten his magic back. Then he'd be called up to the NAPH where he belonged.

I sighed and carefully slipped out of bed, grabbed some sweats out of the closet, and headed downstairs. Morose was not where I wanted to be, and I was very close to ending up there. Time for coffee and a lungful of fresh air.

I brewed up a shot of espresso, then took it and myself outside.

The brisk cold early December air chased away the cobwebs and the thoughts of a future without Drake from my mind. Maybe that would come to be—maybe not. No sense in worrying about it now. Today? Today, the day was bright and despite Drake's very fine work last night, my ass felt fine. A day off with no rain or snow and a bright blue sky? I was getting on my bike.

When I stepped back into the kitchen, a bleary-eyed Drake was at the counter, staring at my espresso machine. "How do you make it work?" There was a plaintive note to the end of that.

"You could've stayed in bed."

"Not without you" was his answer to that.

I'm not sure which warmed me more, the words, or the sharp look he gave me.

"Let me make you something. Espresso? Cappuccino?"

"Just..." He held out his hand like he was holding a mug.

"Okay, sleepyhead. Go sit before you teeter over."

He sniffed, then shuffled to the island's bar stools. "How are you so *happy* this early?"

I brewed up two Americanos. "I woke up next to you."

That seemed to mollify him for a moment. He sipped his coffee and hummed. "But you left."

"Yeah, I know. I got up into my head."

"You?" He actually sounded surprised.

"Me," I said. "Happens sometimes."

Drake put down his coffee mug, then snatched mine from my hand and set that down, too. Then he drew me into a long kiss that had time stopping, my heart pounding, and my dick tenting my sweats. When he broke it, he said, "I know emotions happen. Look at me. I'm kinda a poster child for that. But I hate seeing you sad. Or lonely. What can I do to make you not sad or lonely?"

I felt a wobble in my chest that had everything to do with now *and* the future. But the future wasn't here yet, so I laid my forehead against Drake's. "You've already done that. I'm not sad or lonely with you here."

A sharp, deep, squawk of a meow startled us both, and I looked over to find Loki sitting by our coffee and staring back at me. "Especially not lonely with *that* one around."

Drake laughed and reclaimed his coffee. "Okay, so you have the cats. You have me. Do you want to talk about what's in your head?"

Hmm. He'd opened up about so much to me, the least I could do was open up to him a little. "It's just how I process things. It's like on the ice, except slower because stuff off the ice moves more slowly. I look down the road at all the potential twists and turns and figure out what's going to happen and how I should react." I took a sip of coffee, then continued. "Sometimes I wander too far down the paths and get too deep into the what ifs. Nothing's set. Life can surprise you, but I can't help planning ahead. I don't like not having a plan. Or several. Just in case."

He had that look I'd seen on a lot of other people— where they tried to puzzle me out. "My brain doesn't exactly work in the same way as a lot of other people's."

The corner of his mouth ticked up. "Yeah, I figured that out."

Had he? A lot of people hadn't when they thought they had. "I'm neurodivergent," I said. "I could get into the specifics, but..."

His brow creased. "No, you don't have to, unless you want. I mean—" he gestured around him. "You're very specific about some things, so that makes sense." He leaned against the kitchen island. "You're actually the easiest person I've ever spent this much time with. It's not like anything is a problem—I just don't like seeing you sad."

"I'm not sad, I'm *pensive*."

I sounded peevish, but Drake smiled into his coffee, then glanced at the clock. "I should call my mom. I want to tell her about what happened."

I knew he wasn't talking about the game last night, but about what had happened with the jerk that was his bio father. "That's a good plan. I'll make some breakfast, then I need to head to Hideaway later today—you're welcome to come along."

"On your bike?" His face lit up at that thought.

"You said you'd never driven, right?"

"Yeah, but I've been a passenger before."

Oh God, Mr. Roth, our GM, would be so mad if he found out, but the roads between here and there didn't have much traffic, and it was a dry day— "All right. Call your mom, I'll get us something to eat, and after we clean up ourselves and everything, we can head out."

CHAPTER 9

DRAKE

In the guest room, I stared at my phone. I'd already put the moment off by getting showered and putting on jeans, and a turtleneck I thought clung to my body nicely. It wasn't nightclub clothes, per se. A trip to the bar during the day wasn't anything to get dressed up for, but I wanted to look good for Jon.

I wanted Jon. Wanted to hold and touch him. Share this space with him. Be on the ice. Ride on his bike. Anything. Everything.

I was very, *very* infatuated, and I knew it. But there was something deeper there, too. He talked about not knowing what this was—and I wasn't sure either—except that it was unlike any other relationship I'd been in, ever.

I sighed and turned my phone over. Probably needed to tell mom about that, as well. I sucked in a breath and hit the call button.

A couple rings on the other end, and then my mom picked up. "Hi, honey! Congratulations on the goals last night."

Wait, what? I knew my mom always watched my

NAPH games, but this was the... "Mom, did you get a subscription to the PHL streaming site?"

"Yes?" she said in a tone her generation used when people were being foolish. "Of course I did. I've been watching your games since you were five. I'm not stopping now."

"Technically, I didn't play games at five. At six, yeah, but not five." I'd learned to skate but hadn't picked up a stick yet.

"Haha, don't get smart with me." But she was laughing, so I knew it was fine.

"Thanks. Yeah, it was a good game. Nice to get on the road with the guys. Bus trip—took me back."

"I'm glad you're settling in. Getting your stride."

I was. I wondered if she could see that on the ice. She'd watched me longer than any coach had—always been there for me. "Hey Mom, could you *tell?* That I was doing better?"

There was quiet on the other end of the line, then an exhale. "Yes. When you came out for your first shift, you moved so much better. You have this little hop when you're taking off, and that wasn't there for a while. And when you got the puck, you just—moved like you knew you had it. Rather than like you were worried that you wouldn't keep it. If that makes sense."

It did. I was nodding along, even if she couldn't see me. (She hated video calls.) "No, I understand." I thought about Jon and the questions he'd asked and what unfolded in my head and my therapist...

"I called up that sports psychologist I used to see. I realized I'd bottled something up, and it was affecting me. And I didn't tell you about it, and I probably should've."

"Oh honey, are you okay?" There was an edge of panic

in her voice. "Did something happen on the Lions? Or... or before?"

I knew where her mind had gone. All those stories of abuse. "No no, it's not that. The Lions were fine. No one's hurt me. This was..." I sighed. "So I got some weird messages this summer from a guy claiming he was my father..."

"Oh, he did *not*." Mom's voice dropped into that register that meant she was rolling up her sleeves and curling her hands into fists.

"Yeah," I said, "He did."

I recounted what had happened and my talk with Kara. Everything.

"Fucking money-grubbing asshole," she said, then added. "Sorry, I shouldn't curse, but he makes me so *mad*."

"I hear that word every day, Mom, and more. I'm a hockey player. Cursing's like breathing."

"Yeah, but there are some things you shouldn't hear from your mother."

True. "I didn't want to tell you about him because I didn't want to bring all that up again. I know he was a jerk—and he proved he was a jerk—so why bother you? But—"

"But you should've. Drake, sweetie, the only good thing that ever came from knowing him was you, and I wouldn't change having you for anything in the world. You're the best thing that ever happened to me. I'm just sorry you had to deal with his selfishness. That he couldn't even be a good person—trying to use you as an ATM rather than being *proud*. Fuck that noise." She paused again. "Sorry."

I had to laugh. "I feel a lot better about it—I mean, not great that it happened—but like I can deal with it. I guess that and getting sent down. It made me think that no one wanted me."

"Oh sweetie, you know that's not true."

I thought about Jon downstairs making breakfast. About the coffee he'd made me, and about being with him last night. "I do, yeah." My turn to pause. "Um... I also met someone here."

"Did you?"

Oh, that was the interested mom tone. "Yeah. I went to a queer bar when I got to town, and met this guy. Nothing came of it then, which was probably good, since he's the captain of the Otters."

"Wait, the one that looks like a sexy pirate? Dark hair. Goatee?"

Well, that was one way to describe Jon, I guess. "Mom, ew. But yes."

"Drake, I'm old, not dead, and he's a nice-looking man."

"Again, ew. Stop. But yes, he is. I'm staying with him rather than in a hotel."

"*Oh*," she said, in a knowing way.

"Mom." Ew ew ew.

"Sorry. I'm glad you've met someone you get along with." She sounded like she was trying hard not to laugh.

I gripped my hair with my free hand. "Anyway, I don't know if it'll go anywhere, but he's a really nice guy. I figured I should tell you about my life from time to time, you know?"

"I do appreciate it." The humor was still there, but it fell away. "Especially if it's something I can help you with."

"I'm not sure you can help me with the asshole sperm donor."

She snorted. "Oh, I still have connections. If he gives you any more trouble..."

"Mom," I warned.

"I'm not doing anything. You sound like you have it handled. But if he does something..."

I sighed. "Okay." Then added, "Look, I should go. Jon's making breakfast."

"Okay, sweetie. Good luck with your games, and your boyfriend, too."

God. Boyfriend. I wasn't even sure Jon and I were dating. "Thanks, Mom. Love you."

"Love you, too."

We ended the call, and I tossed the phone onto the bed, scrubbed my face with my hands, then sighed.

Mothers. I loved mine, but boy, they were weird.

Downstairs, I found Jon dancing around the kitchen to music. Sounded like it might be a current-hits mix of some sort, or satellite radio. His face lit up when he saw me, and he told his system to turn itself down. "Just about done."

He'd made...pancakes? Crepes? I couldn't actually tell which. Also eggs, and had put out fresh fruit.

"What are these? I asked, poking at the pancake, then trying a bite, and oh my God. "Shit, these are good."

"Swedish pancakes," he said, then pushed the cut berries over to me. "Put fruit on them."

I did, and I swear I never wanted to leave this house. "It's unfair that you cook this well."

"Is it?" He grinned, then sobered. "How'd your call go?"

"Good. Mom was pissed at jerkface, but not as upset as I thought she might be. More mad that he was bothering me."

Jon nodded.

"And I kind of told her we have a thing."

He raised an eyebrow. "A thing, eh?"

"Yeah, I mean—we do."

He nodded. "I think so, yeah." After eating a little more,

his smile blossomed, and he muttered, as if to himself, "A thing!" in a positively gleeful voice.

My heart tumbled in my chest, so I grabbed my coffee cup. A *thing*, indeed.

BEING ON A MOTORCYCLE WAS EXHILARATING. HAVING a Harley rumbling underneath me while pressed against Jon's back with my arms wrapped around him? Oh my God. Was almost as good as being on the ice, except I wasn't in control. I'd had to give that up to Jon, molding my body to him and shifting my weight when he did as we rode.

I fucking loved it.

We were decked out in leather riding gear, and I had on Jon's spare helmet. We weren't going horribly fast or anything, but I was still ginning ear to ear when we arrived at Hideaway and I took off the helmet.

"Oh," Jon said. "You liked that."

I didn't reply, just clapped him on the shoulder.

He wrapped an arm around my waist and ushered me into the bar—where we were greeted by a long whistle from one of the bikers. "Nice, Jonny."

Jon rolled his eyes. "He wanted to ride on my bike."

"Is that what the kids are calling it these days," Ella quipped.

I laughed. "That was last night."

That got a chorus of *Ooooh* that had Jon rubbing the back of his neck. "Let's leave that alone for now." He turned to me, still smiling. "I need to check on some paperwork. You going to be okay alone for a bit?"

"Sure. How much trouble can I get into here?"

The biker who had teased Jon laughed. "We'll take care of your old man, Jonny."

Jon sighed. "He's younger than me, Red Dog."

"Still your old man," he said.

I was lost. Kind of. "Wait, is that like someone's old woman being their partner?"

"You got it, kiddo," Ella said. To Jon, she said, "Go do your paperwork. He'll be fine."

Jon waved the words away as he headed to his office. "It's not him I'm worried about." He vanished behind a door on the far side of the bar.

The biker, a burly man with red curly hair all over his head and face, patted the stool next to him. "Come on. Sit down and have a beer."

He and his friend, a man with weathered brown skin and black hair, were both older—maybe in their fifties judging by the gray in both their beards and hair—but looked fit and tough. I took the offered seat, and Ella put a pilsner of some kind in front of me. Light enough, but it had a good flavor. "I'm Drake," I said.

"Red Dog," the man said, then indicated to his companion, "And this is Merrick, my deputy."

"Deputy?" Suddenly I was a fish out of water.

Red Dog chuckled. "You don't know much about bikes and bikers."

I shook my head. "Only how to be a passenger, basically."

He grunted. "Jonny'll teach you."

Ella flipped a towel onto her shoulder. "Red Dog here is the president of the Night Bones, his motorcycle club."

That explained the jackets with their rockers. "Is Jon—Jonny—in the club?"

"Nah," Merrick chimed in. "He's got too much on his

plate. Besides, he never rides on the highways if he can help it."

"Hockey," Red Dog said, as if that explained everything. Which it did. "By the way," he added, "nice goals last night. Bet that felt good, getting it behind you."

Oh shit. They knew hockey, too. At least this was a subject I could chat about forever. "Yeah, it did. I was strung out about it before. It's true what they say about gripping your stick too tight and all that."

Both he and Merrick nodded. "Otters are a good team for getting players on track," Merrick said. "Though looks like you didn't need that much to get back to it." He glanced at the office door.

I laughed. Couldn't help it. Then I sipped my beer and grinned. "He's a good man."

They both seemed to agree with that.

"So," Red Dog said, "What do you think is going on with Washington? Their goalie was so damn hot, but they just lost nine to one."

I'd caught that in the news, but hadn't looked into it. "I'd have to see the video to know for sure, but sometimes everyone on the team has the worst day on the ice at the same time, and it snowballs out of control. One goal against becomes three, becomes six and it just *sucks* if you're the losing team." I shook my head. "Those are the games you absolutely have to forget. Like, move on. It's worse for the goalies because a lot of times, it's not their fault, you know? Gotta play well in front of them. But they take the blame and the stats hit."

By the time Jon came back, we were deep into a discussion about how you flush a bad game, how you make it up to a goaltender, and some of the psychology behind momentum swings.

Jon raised an eyebrow when he took a seat. "I go away for a half hour, and you're talking *this* with *them*?" He shook his head in mock disgust. "Honestly."

Merrick slapped Jon on the back. "Kid's smart. Like you."

Red Dog nodded slowly. "Good choice."

I think both of us went a little flush. "For him or me?" Jon asked.

"Yes," Red Dog said.

I probably shouldn't have felt as happy about that proclamation as I did, but there it was. Jon and me—we were something good. And more and more, that something looked like a couple.

CHAPTER 10

JON

While I enjoyed a white Christmas, I was grateful for no snow *this* Christmas Eve, as it allowed all my teammates to park in my driveway and on my lawn. The annual party was easy to set up—everyone brought a dish, dessert, or beverage, a small kid's present if they were bringing a child, and a white elephant gift. All the kids got random good presents, and we spent time eating, unwrapping, and stealing each other's awful presents.

Drake was a saint, from helping with the pre-party cleaning, to being out there in the cold, parking everyone, to organizing the food while I played host. Made an easy process even easier.

There was one deviation from the script this year, though. Both Alfie and Ebba had mentioned to me that they were grateful for a Christmas Eve party because they were horribly homesick for Sweden this time of year. I kind of understood. I'd grown up in North America and my mother was Canadian, but my dad and the other Swedish players would take turns being Saint Nick on Christmas Eve to show up at each other's houses to surprise us kids, and our house hadn't been an exception. I'd grown up with a lot of the Swedish traditions.

Alfie and Ebba didn't have kids, but I figured the other children in the house wouldn't mind a visit from Saint Nick, so halfway through the night, I stole out to my very frigid shed and donned a Santa suit and beard and waltzed back in. The hardest part was trying to maintain a Norwegian accent in Swedish. Especially given that my Swedish accent was American-tinged.

Still, the look on Ebba and Alfie's faces made the stunt worthwhile. They were both so incredibly happy and Ebba was in tears with laughter. And the kids at the party? They were screeching with joy, especially since they all got another round of gifts, since what Santa doesn't bring presents?

When the night wound down, and they were getting ready to head home, Ebba pulled me into a hug. "Thank you. A little touch of home."

"The least I can do." I gave her a squeeze and patted Alfie on the back. "Your turn next year. I'll let you borrow the suit."

He laughed at that.

Ebba gave Drake a hug, too, and switched to English. "You take care of him. He's a treasure."

"I know," he said. "And I will. Promise."

God, my heart. "I'm not—"

Alfie shushed me. "Don't argue with Ebba on Christmas." His smile was bright. "God Jul, Jon."

"God Jul," I called after them.

Drake wrapped an arm around my waist. "You *are* a treasure," he said. "And don't argue with guests."

I wrinkled my nose at him. "You're not a guest," I said before my brain caught up with what I was saying.

Both of his eyebrows lifted. "Oh?" There was a hint of a smile on his lips. "Tenant, then? Roommate?"

Fine. I'd say it. "Boyfriend."

"Ooooh. Boyfriend." He pulled me close and stole a kiss. "Don't argue with your boyfriend."

Mac slapped me on my back and pushed a little yelp out of me.

"Kid's right. Don't argue with him." Then Mac was gone, out the door, too, leaving me startled and laughing out of sheer reflex.

Drake was grinning like he'd won the jackpot. Maybe we both had.

After everyone headed home, I grabbed my phone and jiggled it at Drake. "Going to call my parents."

His eyebrows rose. "This late?" It was almost midnight.

"Well, they're in Vancouver, so..."

"Right. Time zones. Duh."

I chuckled, then dialed, and my father answered.

"Hej Pappa, God Jul."

"God Jul, son. Hur mår du?"

I laughed, because the answer to that was nearly always the same. "Bra, bra, du?"

"I'm fine, so's your mother, but I'm sure she'll fill you in on all those details later. Team's doing well, I see. Beautiful goal the other night."

Of course Papa watched every game of mine that he could. "All I had to do was put my blade down. That was all Drake."

And of course Papa disagreed. "Williams certainly was a major component, but I saw your backcheck and passing to set that up. For someone convinced that they're not a good skater, you flew up the ice." Humor laced his words.

I rolled my eyes, paced from the kitchen to the living

room and flopped onto the couch. "That's not good skating, that's fast skating. Anyone can do that." I sounded more like a teen than an adult.

"Jon." His admonishment was gentle and full of love. "You know that's not true."

I sighed. "Okay, yes. I helped set the play, and I knew where I needed to go if it worked, but it was Drake who made that happen. I don't think there's another guy on the team who could've gotten around their D like he did."

"That's better," he said. "And yes, you're right. It's also good to see Williams get his swagger back. Kid's going to be quite the star in a year or two."

Drake, puttering around the kitchen called out, "It's kind of rude to talk about someone in a language they don't understand."

I gave Drake a look, and said, "I'm telling my father that goal the other day was all you, that's all."

"It was not! You're the one that set up the breakout and got to the net! That was all you!"

In my ear, my father started laughing. "Give him the phone for a moment."

I stood, paced to the kitchen and held out my phone to Drake. "My father wants to speak to you."

That made his eyebrows arch so high, I thought they might fly off his face, but he took the phone. "Hello, sir." A pause. "Gunner."

Yeah, Papa hated being called sir. Absolutely convinced he was just some dude, not a hall-of-famer everyone looked up to.

"No, I know." Drake's gaze met mine. "He's so smart out there." The smile that slid onto Drake's face lit up my world. "Yes." Another look at me. "I will. Thank you, Gunner."

Then Drake handed the phone back to me. "Your dad's nice."

"Mmmhmm." I put the phone to my ear. "Papa."

"You hear that? Your papa is nice."

I stuck my tongue out at Drake, then spoke. "I've never ever said you weren't!"

That got me another bark of laughter, then Papa sobered. "Your Drake is nice, too."

I took a deep breath. "I know. Papa—" I paused. "You know when you met Mom..."

"Oh," he said. "Jon."

"Yeah. Only, I don't know what I'm going to do when..." I waved my hand, fully aware that he couldn't see me, but Drake could, and the latter was looking at me with creased brows. But Papa understood. He knew Drake would get called up eventually.

"Jon," he said. "You'll do what your heart tells you to do. You'll do what you need to. If you love him like I love your mother, you'll walk off the end of the world for him."

I turned away from Drake as moisture welled in my eyes. "Yeah, it's like that."

"Good," Papa said. "You deserve someone who makes your heart sing."

My laugh had a little choke to the edge of it. I knew Drake was watching me, but I didn't turn around until I was sure I wasn't going to lose it. When I did, I smiled—and he relaxed.

"Speaking of your mother—" Papa said.

Then Mom's voice sounded in my ear. "So, tell me about this young man of yours!"

This time, my laugh was higher. And then I expounded on all Drake's virtues—in English—and watched him blush, then drop his head into his hands.

"Okay, okay, you can go back to talking in Swedish."

"Mom's Canadian." I said as I sat back down on the couch.

He threw his hands up and headed into the kitchen to snag a leftover cookie.

"I've driven him to sweets," I said to Mom.

"You're just like your father."

Our conversation after that was more about family—how my cousins and my sister were doing. Sofia wasn't with them this Christmas, but with her partner's family. Then Mom filled me in with the various goings on of neighbors and funny stories from Papa's charity events. "You need to come out here this summer. Your father and I would love to see you. Bring Drake, too."

I didn't know if Drake had summer plans. I didn't know if we'd even be together by summer, what with him likely back on the Lions roster by then. I didn't say that, though. "The bar—"

"Can take care of itself. Aren't you always praising Ella? Saying you should see if she wants to buy in?"

I scratched the back of my head. "Okay. We'll see what we can swing."

"Good. I want to meet this man of yours. There's only so much you can glean from pointless interviews about getting pucks deep and playing on your toes."

I laughed, because Mom knew. She'd had years of listening to Papa answer media, and not much had changed in terms of canned answers.

We chatted a little longer, then I wrapped the conversation up and ended the call, since it was now past midnight, and while we had Christmas off, we'd be back at it the day after.

And I had a little planning to do for a few days after

that—because Drake's birthday was coming up and I wanted to finally go on that dinner date we'd meant to go on before we'd fallen into bed.

Evidently, Drake also had more plans for tonight, because he came to a halt in front of me, hands on his hips. "You done?"

I peered up at him. "Yeah."

"Good. Because It's Christmas, and there's a package I want to unwrap."

I burst out laughing at the cheese in *that* line. Absolutely ridiculous when combined with his try at a leering expression, given those innocent blue eyes and that curly blond hair. Like the elf they put on shelves trying to be sexy.

The joy in me shook my whole body, and I had to pull my knees to my chest. I ended up sideways, trying to gulp for air as tears caught in the corners of my eyes.

Drake sputtered into laughter and ended up kneeling by the couch. We both calmed down, but then I snickered and said, "Package," and we were both gone again.

"God," Drake said, as he wiped his eyes. "I fucking love you."

My breath caught. "Yeah?"

"Yeah." He put his hands on his thighs. "Yeah. Merry Christmas, Jon. I love you."

I tipped myself upright. "That's the best present I could get."

The way Drake looked at me... Felt like my chest might burst open from happiness. "Yeah?" he said again, this time with a grin that was twinkling more than the lights on the Christmas tree.

Fuck yes. "C'mere." I beckoned him forward with my index finger and when he was close enough, pulled him into a hard kiss that I hoped left no questions about how I felt.

But just in case, I spoke between devouring his lovely mouth. "I love you, too."

"Oh. Good. Does that mean you'll take me upstairs and unwrap me?"

I smiled against his mouth. "Absolutely."

Unwrap. Taste. Feel. Fuck. Love. I did all I could to make Drake understand just how much I loved him.

THE DAY BEFORE DRAKE'S BIRTHDAY, WE PLAYED AT home, thank goodness. No road trip meant I could plan the next day carefully. I was utterly grateful the scheduling had worked out to my advantage. As it was, today had been nice so far—one of those uneventful late December days. Cold and gray. The roads were dry, but that could change. There was a hint of smoke in the air, and that made it feel like it might snow.

After our morning practice, we took my truck over to the bar. I had some end-of-the-year bookkeeping to do and wanted to make sure we were all set for New Year's Eve, especially since we'd play a game that night, too.

New Year's Eve was one of Hideaway's busiest nights of the year, since we were a safe place for local queer people. I'd witnessed more kisses and proposals on the last night of the year than I could count. It was always a night full of hope and music, dancing, laughter, and love.

This year, after the game, I'd get to experience that with Drake, with my boyfriend. That thought was enough to make me giddy.

But for New Year's to be a success, I needed to do a little work, especially since tomorrow was all about Drake.

"Are you sure you don't mind hanging out while I do paper-work? I could drop you at the house."

"It's fine."

I couldn't tell his tone, so I hazarded a quick glance over, but his expression was unreadable, too. "You okay?"

"Huh?" He shook himself. "Yeah, yeah. Sorry. No, I love the bar. It's just..." He trailed off, and the silence stretched out for longer than I liked before he heaved a sigh. "Jerkface messaged me to wish me a happy birthday."

"Ah, fuck. I thought you had him blocked?"

"I did." He shook himself. "I shouldn't let it get to me." He ticked points off on his fingers. "Number one, he got the date wrong. Two, he disregarded my boundaries. Three, he's an asshole. Four—" He paused and dropped his hands to his lap. "Four, I'm here with you and we're going to the bar. Red Dog said next time he and I were both there, he'd play a game of pool with me."

Oh God. I bit my lip as I turned onto the road that led to the bar. "Don't bet on that game. Red Dog will want you to, and then he'll clean your wallet out."

"Is he that good?"

I huffed a laugh. "Oh yeah. He'll pretend he isn't at first, but that man must've been a pool shark in his past."

A few moments later, I pulled my truck into the farthest spot from the door. Red Dog's Indian was with a pack of other bikes I recognized from Red Dog's club. Bunch of cars in the lot, too. Pretty nice crowd for a Sunday afternoon.

Indeed the place was packed, and over the loud conversations about the football game on the TVs, Merrick called out "Jonny boy!" and there was even more noise as various people called my name. I saw Drake smiling when Red Dog gestured to him to join the crew.

I caught his elbow. "Don't lose all your money!"

He laughed. "I won't," he said, then kissed me. Just a peck, but on the lips and in public. Sure, we were in a queer bar, so no worries there, but it was *my* queer bar so the hooting and hollering had my face uncomfortably warm in no time flat.

I headed to the end of the bar where Lorelei, one of my weekend bartenders, was serving. She was an older white woman with hair that changed color at whim. Like Ella, she took no shit from anyone.

Ella was busy at the other end, near Red Dog's crew—and Drake. She said something to Drake, and I took a moment to drink in his smile as he bantered back.

"That young man really has you taken, doesn't he?" Lorelei said. She handed me a glass of water.

"What? I mean...yes?" Embarrassment crept back into my body. "I guess it shows, huh?"

"Honey, you look at him like he's your moon."

Well, shit. I scratched the back of my head. "He's something else."

"You're something else, too." She shook her head. "You two almost make me wish I were in my twenties again." She paused. "But then I'd be Larry, and I have less than no desire to be him again." She smiled. "Besides, Stephen has been amazing."

Stephen was her latest boyfriend. A truck driver for a local company. "Well, I'm glad you're here now, and you." I pointed to the back office. "Need to go check on stuff for New Year's."

She scoffed. "You only love me because I keep this place sane during the rush."

"Well, yes. That and your stunning personality, beauty, and your vast knowledge of cocktails."

She laughed. I gave her a wave and headed into the

back. It took me less time than I thought to wrap up the books for the year. We were all set for supplies as far as I could tell. Tomorrow, we'd get a delivery of beer and spirits, and the remaining supplies we needed for a killer party. The DJ was a regular, and I'd hired a few extra hands for the night—all folks that had worked the party before.

I was always nervous about big events here. Part of it was business—these things were easy enough to screw up—but part was also that underlying worry about gathering that many queer people into one location. The Hideaway was off the beaten path, yes, but not unknown. College kids found us. Businesspeople found us. Every so often a bigot showed up—and it only took one with ugly intent to turn a party into a tragedy.

But celebration was defiance, so we would dance and sing and drink and party into the night.

When I headed back out into the bar, I stopped to soak in the surroundings. This place had come a long way in the years since I first stepped into it, and then took over. We operated in the black. We had regulars. We had good staff. This place practically ran without me.

Which was good, since the Otters did take most of my time during the season, as they should. And Drake was occupying more and more of my free time. When he got recalled to the Lions—I shook my head to clear it. We'd cross that bridge. In the meantime, there were things I could set into motion to make sure the Hideaway was properly cared for in the years to come, whether I was here or not.

Hockey was a game where you lived in the moment, but you needed to be able to see a couple moves ahead. I had a sense of game flow and what plays might happen, both on and off the ice.

That moment, standing at the back of the Hideaway,

watching Drake try to beat Red Dog at pool while Ella and Lorelei slung drinks at the bar and a football game flashed on the screens—well, it felt like one of those moments where I knew what was coming.

I didn't know exactly when it would happen, but change? I felt that in my bones.

I suppose that pensive nature of mine—my need to plan—had me more quiet than usual during our ride back to the house. Drake filled my silence with the tale of him beating Red Dog at pool on a very lucky shot, and some of the other antics of Hideaway's patrons. When we got into the house, he pulled me into his arms.

"Hey, everything okay with the bar?"

I leaned into his warmth and wrapped my arms around him. "Mmmhmm. Everything's set for New Year's."

He and I stood like that in the foyer for a while. Thor rubbed against our legs and Loki squawked from the platform on his scratching post.

Drake chuckled. "Snack time for big kitty." But he didn't move. "Do you need to talk?"

I pressed my nose against the crook of his neck and inhaled the clean smell from his shower gel. "It's almost midseason."

He pulled back a little and eyed me. "You think the Lions are going to call me back up."

"I know they will. It's a matter of when."

He took my hands in his and kissed each one in turn. "Pittsburgh's not that far. We'll figure things out."

Which meant he wanted to keep this going when that happened. Weight off my shoulders. "I'm glad you want to figure things out."

His brow creased for a moment, then he chuckled. "Of course I want to."

"I mean—" I shrugged. "I'm an old man who's about to get older. I'm sure a hot guy like you could—" He tickled me. "Hey!" I danced away, laughing.

He regathered me into his arms. "There is no one like you, Jon. No one on this planet I'd rather be with."

Well, shit. "I guess that's a good thing, eh?"

His laugh was exasperated. "Come on, let's get a nap before we have to leave for the game." Then he pulled me upstairs.

———

WE LOST THE GAME IN OVERTIME, AND THAT WAS probably the first sign that the next twenty-four hours wouldn't go the way I'd planned them. The second sign was the three inches of snow that had fallen while we'd been in the arena, with more accumulating as we walked out.

We had to be careful navigating the parking lot in our dress shoes. Drake wrinkled his nose. "Was it supposed to snow?"

"A little, I think. A dusting?"

Drake climbed into my truck. "This is *not* a dusting."

It absolutely was not. The flakes were big and falling fast, and there was already a Winter Storm Warning in effect. Somehow, the weather had gone from less than a half an inch to eight to twelve inches in the hours we'd been in the arena.

The traffic on the roads home was light, which was good, since they were a fucking mess. Even Route 30, which should've gotten some attention from the plows, was a nightmare. I was glad to have the truck—with relatively new tires, too.

"Fucking hell," Drake muttered as we passed a car struggling to make it up one of the hills. "This isn't good."

I grunted and focused all of my concentration on getting us back to the house. It was easier once we'd gotten off the main roads. The back roads were completely untreated, and if you didn't know how they went, they might have been hard to drive, but the truck packed the snow down well enough to get reasonable traction, and I knew every curve. I had to drive slowly, so it took a while, but I got us back to the house, safe and sound.

Still, once I turned the engine off, my body shook, and I slumped back against the driver's seat. Drake blew out a breath. "This is wild," he said, looking around at the snow that was still coming down. "Holy shit."

"I don't want to do that again," I murmured. "Not for a while." I pushed open the door. "Let's get in where it's warm."

The cats sniffed at the snow we dragged into the foyer, where we shed our coats and shoes. My socks were damp, and I hated that, so I took them off right there. "Going to throw these in the laundry and change into something more comfortable."

Drake followed me—he'd moved some of his things into my bedroom, since we spent every night since our first in my bed. The sex was awesome, but we both had confessed that we liked sleeping with each other. The cats approved, too, having all their humans in one room.

And Drake was very much one of their humans. He was, at least for now, *my* human, too.

After we'd changed into sweats, I waved my hand in the direction of the kitchen. "Tea?"

He chaffed his hands together. "Please."

The truck had been warm and the house was fine, but

there was something about tonight that was icy—the snow, the loss—I didn't know what.

As I waited for the kettle to boil, I looked out into the backyard. There was only white and dark. Snow and the night. There had to be four or five inches by now, and it showed no signs of stopping. The weather app on my phone had dark blue bands over the area and we were now under a Blizzard Warning.

There went any plans I had for tomorrow. Well, not true—just the parts that I'd planned outside of the house. "I had a dinner reservation for tomorrow," I said. "For your birthday."

Drake pulled two mugs out of the cabinet, and one of the evening blends of herbal tea I kept around. "Oh," he said. "So it's your fault it's snowing?" He almost dead-panned that, but the twitch at the corner of his lips gave him away, and it only took me giving him a look for the grin to appear. "Kidding. But at this rate, we're never getting that date."

"Even the weather conspires against us." I shook my head and poured water into the mugs. We settled in on the couch with our mugs and a blanket, and in no time, had two cats joining us. "I had *plans*, too. There's a French place in Pittsburgh..." I waved at the windows. "We are not driving to Pittsburgh tomorrow. The Turnpike might be fine, but the roads around here and in the city are going to be a *mess*."

Drake put his mug on the coffee table and snuggled up against me. "An entire day lazing with you sounds like the perfect birthday."

Yeah, that wouldn't be so bad. I sipped my tea, then wrapped my arm around him. "I did plan to make you breakfast. I guess I'm making lunch and dinner now, too."

"We can build a snowman."

I blinked, grinned, and started singing "Do you want to..."

Fingers over my lips stopped me. "Don't!" Drake said. "You'll get that stuck in my head!"

"Okay, fine. I'll let it go, then."

"Ugh. If you weren't holding a mug of hot liquid with Thor right there, I'd tickle you." Still, Drake brushed over the sensitive spot on my side.

"So glad you're concerned about the cat," I took another gulp of tea. "And now I know where I fall in the pecking order."

"Pretty sure Loki already told you that."

He had a point. I set my mug down next to his. "Oh, Loki told me that years ago. Thor, too. But I thought I was a little higher on your list.

He shifted on the couch, and rotated so he could push himself up and kiss me. "You are very *high* on my list," he whispered against my lips.

Holding Drake was so easy, and we fit so well together. "Yeah? You like me more than Thor? Loki? Chocolate pancakes?"

I got another kiss for my answer, then another. It didn't take very long for Drake to go from snuggling against me to laying on top of me, his hard length pressing into my thigh. "I love you more than chocolate, cats, *and* coffee." He took my mouth again, and I savored his spectacular kisses and his weight pressing me into the couch. "Come upstairs with me, and I'll show you exactly how much."

Well, I wasn't one to say no to *that*.

CHAPTER 11

DRAKE

Jon had warned me that the New Year's Eve game was always a riot, in both good and bad ways, and he'd been exactly right. It was a high-scoring, back-and-forth affair with a shit-ton of penalties, hits, and scrums breaking out at every whistle.

I'd been paired up with Jon and Alfie again, and our line kept scoring on the other team. We'd each put a goal into the net, and I'd added another.

Unfortunately we were tied at five each. This time, when we went out, their biggest D-man, who had to be six-five, went after Alfie, and had sent him flying into the boards. I saw red in that moment, rammed into the guy, and asked him if he wanted to go.

He did, so the gloves came off and we squared up. He had height on me, and weight, but I was angrier than I'd been in a while, and I'd always been shifty in fights. He missed connecting his swings. I did *not* and I was able to get in close enough to tangle him up and take him down.

Of course that put both of us in the box for five. Not

ideal, but our team and fans were yelling and cheering, and Alfie seemed to be okay.

Jon looked—he looked like he wanted to obliterate the other team. I'd never seen him that sharp and dangerous-looking on the ice. There was fire in him on the bench, I watched from the penalty box as he talked with Alfie and Bruda. When they hopped over the boards, along with our biggest D-men, they went to work with spectacular results. Alfie took vengeance, skating around their lumbering D, then passing to Bruda, who sent the puck up to Jon, who wound up and one-timed the puck from the hashmarks straight past the goalie. I was almost surprised the netting didn't explode from the force when the puck hit.

I'd never seen Jon shoot a puck like that. You could barely hear our goal song over the shouts and yells of the fans. I was on my feet, too.

I got out of the box with a minute thirty-seven left on the clock, and on my shift, worked to keep the score six to five, even with their goalie pulled for the extra man. We didn't get the insurance empty netter, but we did keep their pucks out of our net and won.

The arena was so loud. Jon got first star that night. I got second, and Alfie got third. The locker room was almost as loud as the arena had been, and we whooped it up, even as Jon and I tried to get cleaned up and shoved some food into ourselves so we could get over to the bar.

We managed to make it there just after eleven, and wow, the place was packed. A cheer went up when we walked in.

"Stars!" someone yelled. "The stars are here!"

Lots of pats on the back, including from Red Dog. "You're tough, kid. Taking on a big guy like that."

"That hit on Alfie." I shook my head. "Wasn't right. Had to send a message."

Merrick nodded in approval. Jon looked consternated but didn't say anything, so I filed his expression away. That was something we needed to discuss later.

Ella got us beers, and we made our way around the place, talking with the people we knew. The pool queens fussed over me a little, making sure "that nasty man" hadn't bruised my "pretty face," with me assuring them that he hadn't touched me. When we moved on, I pulled Jon into a little pocket of calm in the sea of chaos. "Hey, you're not mad at me, are you?"

That got me Jon's confused look. "*Mad* at you? Why would I be mad at you?"

"For fighting tonight."

"For fighting? No, no. I mean, I would hate seeing you get hurt in a fight, but honestly, I was about to do the same thing. You got there sooner." Jon paused. "And probably did a better job anyway." He shook his head. "I'm still angry at that ass targeting Alfie and the refs only calling the fighting major. That was *clearly* interference. Pisses me off." His features smoothed out. "Usually, I can shake that off, you know? Bad calls. But..."

"But it's Alfie?"

Jon scratched his head. "Yeah. He's like a little brother, I guess."

I could see that. "He's our teammate. That's why I dropped the gloves."

That got me a smile from Jon. "You said 'our.'"

"I did." And I'd meant it.

That smile didn't leave Jon's face until close to midnight.

As the seconds counted down, he took my hand and

that smile shifted to something far more serious, and I found myself staring into his dark eyes. We didn't say anything when the count passed ten—just watched each other as the time from one year ticked to another. We moved toward each other right before everyone screamed *one*, then we kissed. Not as passionately as we might before sex, but intently, as if each of us was memorizing how our bodies, how our lips molded together in that moment. Cheers went up all around us, along with bells and horns. People threw confetti and, as we separated, bits of colored paper fell around us, clinging to our hair and clothes. That joyful smile was back as others jostled Jon and wished him a happy New Year. I was pulled into more hugs than I could count, including one from Red Dog.

"You be good to him, you hear?"

"I— I will be." That was the only answer I had, because it was the truth. I'd be as good as I could be to Jon.

Red Dog nodded, and he moved on. The pool queens enveloped me next.

Eventually, Jon and I ended up together against the back wall, by the pool tables, and he slumped against me. "That was fantastic. Just look at everyone!" He gestured out at the bar where so many people were gathered. Feathers, leather, rainbows, glitter, and confetti were everywhere. It was a sight to behold. Lorelei was excitedly talking to an older man while clutching his hands.

"Hey, did Lorelei get engaged?" I asked.

"I think so?" Jon pulled me off the wall. "Let's go find out."

We worked our way through the crowd, and indeed, Lorelei had gotten engaged to an older gentleman named Stephen, and she was just gushing. We congratulated the lucky couple.

"Maybe," she said, "Next year, it'll be you two."

My heart tumbled in my chest, and Jon got that look again that stole away his smile. "Maybe," he said. Then the joy returned and he grinned at me. "Maybe?"

I took his hand and kissed his knuckles. "We'll see."

There was so much time between now and then. So many seconds, as they say. I had no idea what would happen, and it might be tough, given the way hockey was, but if we could stay together, we could stay together.

Maybe.

THE COUPLE OF DAYS AFTER THE FIRST OF JANUARY HAD been beautiful, with pale winter skies and the brilliant snow-covered hills contrasting against the browns and grays of the leafless trees and the dark greens of the pines. On the day before Jon's birthday, the roads were dry and the early morning sunlight shown through another clear day. No repeat of blizzard conditions in the forecast, which was good, because we had an away game.

The trip to Cincinnati was uneventful. We walked into their arena and came out with a win. A nice four to two in regulation. Coach Macintosh held us back while people were filing out of the arena to the bus.

"You," he said, pointing to Jon. "If you're going to go for those fancy passes through traffic up ice, please make sure the guy you're passing to is actually expecting the puck."

Jon shrugged unapologetically. "Riley needs to have better situational awareness in the game. Not everything is about hitting the guy in front of him."

Coach rolled his eyes. "Yes. But you know what he's like. Do a pass like that when Alfie or this kid is out, okay?"

Jon nodded. That pass and Riley's fumbling of it had let Cincinnati tie the game at two each. It'd been my goal that had put us up in the end, and an empty-netter sealed the deal.

Coach clapped me on the back "You keep playing like you do. I swear, any of these guys could throw a pass to you near the net, and you'd put it in."

"I still have room to improve, Coach. But I'll keep it up."

"Do that." He nodded, then waved toward the exit.

We glanced at each other, then headed to the bus. Jon went first, then abruptly stopped when everyone on the bus yelled, "Happy Birthday!"

"Oh my God," Jon said.

I peeked around him, and there were tinsel streamers everywhere, and banners that said HAPPY 30TH BIRTHDAY! along with ones that read OVER THE HILL.

Jon rotated to me, his eyes wide.

Mine were pretty damn wide, too. "I didn't do this." I hadn't. The vibe I was going for was romantic. And this? It wasn't that. This was teammates talking shit.

"I believe you," he said. "I'm gonna kill Mac."

Then he looked at the rest of our teammate and shook his head. "I hate you all." He was beaming from ear to ear.

The ride home was loud. There was cake and party hats, and even noisemakers. Alfie and Bruda owned up to planning the surprise, and they confirmed I hadn't known, because they didn't think I'd be able to keep a secret. Mac had held us back to give them time to set up.

"I figure you have something romantic planned," Alfie said to me.

I shrugged. "Maybe." But I couldn't quite keep the smile off my face. Jon bumping me and his grin didn't help. "Not that I'm telling you yet," I said to him.

I'd made a reservation at a local restaurant—not the fancy French place in Pittsburgh, but a nice brew pub with lots of beers on tap and a really good menu right in Greensburg. I figured we'd finally have that date, then come home, watch a movie, and spend the rest of the time in bed. Since that first night, I'd been topping him exclusively. Given the way he moaned and cried and came, I knew he liked that, but he'd also said he was vers.

And well, sometimes I liked being on the receiving end. So, I was going to see if he wanted to change things up for his birthday.

I was not about to announce that to our teammates, though.

The drive back to Jon's was quiet and calm and he spent the scant minutes smiling as if he couldn't stop. "I love that team," he said, "so so much. The guys are good to me, even when they're being absolute shits."

I chuckled. "Best kind of team."

"Yeah. So lucky I ended up here. The Otters. Hideaway. Everyone. It's far from my parents, but this is home, you know? These people. This place."

I nodded, a little lump forming in my throat. He was right. This place did feel like home. But that was because of Jon. *He* felt like home. "I love you," I murmured.

"Oh," he said, breathlessly, as if I'd spoken something profound, as if we hadn't said it many times since Christmas. Since our kiss on New Year's. "That's the best gift I've ever received."

He pulled into his driveway and parked, then pulled me into a kiss. "I love you too," he said against my lips.

I grinned like a fool. "Is it after midnight, yet?" It had to be something closer to one, actually.

He checked his watch. "Yup." Just a single word. So unusual for him.

"We should go inside."

Same grin. "Yup."

Oh, I *see*. There were two versions of Jon when horny: Talks a mile a minute and vibratingly quiet. Looks like I had the latter tonight.

In the foyer of Jon's house, I didn't even wait to shuck our coats before I pulled him into a long kiss that left both of us breathless and him dazed. "Happy birthday, Jon."

"Very," he said.

I helped him take his coat off, then hung his and mine in the closet. "I had a thought for tonight."

He licked his lips, and I wondered if he was still tasting my kiss. "You want to try something new?"

I took his mouth in another kiss, sipping and nipping until he melted against me. He'd been wearing burgundy and black tonight, which was such a hot look on him. Then again, everything Jon wore looked great on him. Probably because he was just so beautiful, he could've made a plastic garbage bag look sexy. I worked his tie loose.

"I'll do anything you want," he murmured. "Well, within reason. No maiming or injuring or weird internet dances."

I chuckled. "I'm not asking you to do a TikTok meme, I'm asking if you want to top me tonight."

Those big brown eyes of his widened, and then I was the one up against the wall. His mouth was a firebrand on mine, even as his fingertips caressed my face. This was more like what I'd initially expected from Jon—in control. Strong.

He broke the kiss, then ran his thumb over my lip. "I absolutely can top you." He nodded toward the stairs. "Bedroom?"

Didn't have to ask me twice. We went to his—more ours now—and he slowly stripped me of my suit, then peeled off his. It was a careful, teasing dance of touch and tastes. Kisses, licks, and bites. Insistent, but gentle.

"How do you want this to go?" he asked as he nipped his way down my neck. "What's your fantasy?"

This. This was my fantasy. Being with him in any capacity. "It's your birthday. Whatever you want."

"Mmm, whatever I want? Okay. I can work with that."

What I thought I'd get was more demanding kisses, like the one he'd given me downstairs. Instead, Jon continued to peel clothes off of me until I was naked, then slowly made out with me. It was passionate and feverishly hot, but so careful and thorough. I think he kissed, sucked, and touched every inch of my body before he laid me out on the bed. Then he worshiped me all over again.

"Jon. You're gonna kill me."

There was that laugh I loved. "Baby, I'm going to do worse than that—I'm going to make love to you."

And he did. All those touches and kisses, the way he lovingly sucked my dick and balls. How he opened me with slick fingers, all the while cataloging how stunning I looked, how beautifully I moved. It was all love. Over and over again, he showed me with his body, his words, and the way he looked at me—as if I were the only living being left in the world.

When he finally pressed into me, I was so far gone, I could only hold on and let him love me, over and over, until I was on the edge of what felt to be the most sublime orgasm of my life. "Babe, oh God, babe."

"That's it, he murmured. "Just like that. Want to see you come for me, baby."

I did. So hard that I couldn't even shout. Everything Jon

did took my breath away. By the time I came back down to Earth, he was caressing my face again, much like he had downstairs.

"I love you so much," he whispered. "Thank you."

"You... you..." I struggled to put my thoughts into words. "You're perfect."

"Hardly." His soft chuckle was the last thing I heard before I fell asleep.

MY PHONE RINGING WOKE ME UP AT WAY-TOO-EARLY IN the morning. There were very few numbers I had set to break through my do not disturb setting, so I knew it was important. I just prayed it wasn't my mom. She wouldn't call this early after a road trip unless...

But it wasn't my mom. My phone said *JR*. It took me only a second to remember who *that* was. I answered as Jon stirred next to me and rubbed his eyes.

"Hello, sir."

Our GM replied, "Ah, good. You're awake. I know you had a late night of travel. Congratulations on the win, by the way."

"Thank you, sir." I had no idea why JR would be calling me at—I peered at a decorative but functional wall clock— five to eight in the morning.

Who? Jon mouthed.

JR, I mouthed back, and Jon's eyes got wide.

In my ear, JR continued. "Bear's gone down with a high-ankle sprain. Going to be out for a while. We're recalling you to the Lions. You've put in the work down there. You're the best player the Otters have right now, and we need your talent and skill. You up for that, kid?"

Oh my God. I was getting called up. Going back to the NAPH. I hesitated for a moment, then blurted out, "Yes, sir. Thank you for the challenge."

"That's what I like to hear. Morning skate's at ten thirty at the arena. I'll tell Robinson to expect you. Impress me tonight." Then he hung up.

I pulled the phone away from my ear and stared at it, because I still wasn't sure I'd heard what he'd said correctly. "I'm getting called up."

"Yeah," Jon said gently. "I figured." His smile was small, and it almost hid the sadness in his eyes.

Then it hit me. "It's your birthday." I shook my head. "I can't go. I have plans." The phone shook in my hands.

As I made to call JR back, Jon snatched the phone away and shut it off. "What? No! Don't be foolish. This is what you've been waiting for! You belong on the Lions."

"I belong with you!"

The words echoed around his room, then hung between us, with all the weight of truth and love.

"I can't leave you." I said more quietly. "I don't want to leave you."

"Babe." He breathed the word out, then sat up and put my phone on the nightstand, next to his. "You need to go back to Pittsburgh and play on the Lions and be the super-star you were becoming last season. It's the right thing. The Otters are fun, but we can't further your career."

"I don't care about my career!"

He took both my shaking hands and gave them a squeeze. "You do. And you will, when you get over the shock."

He didn't want me here? "I thought..." I pulled my hands from his. "So it's just—what? Goodbye?"

He looked at me as if I'd started speaking another

language he didn't understand. "No?" Then his face flitted from bewildered to understanding, to exasperation. "Oh my God, Drake." With that, he pulled me into a hug. "We're not breaking up. You're going to play on the Lions, like you're supposed to. We can still see each other, still date. All of that." He pulled back. "Just—we won't be living with each other. It'll be like a more normal relationship, I guess. You know, where people have to schedule things and all that..."

My aching heart ticked down a notch. "You mean like the dinner date we still haven't managed? The one I was finally going to take you on for your birthday?" Jon still wanted me. That was—that was good, right?

This time, Jon's smile was its normal brightness, as was his laugh. "Hell, we might actually manage an actual dinner date if we're not living together." He nodded toward the bathroom. "Why don't you take a shower? I'll get coffee going. Guarantee you'll feel better and things won't look so dire once we chase away the sleep from your head. This is *good news*, babe. Don't you worry about us. There's nothing to worry about."

"But—your birthday."

"Shower," he said with finality.

So I got my ass out of bed and headed to do that.

He was right, the shower helped chase away some of the cobwebs, and the confusion and worry seeped away to be replaced by exhilaration. Holy shit, I was going back up! I had to go get my gear. Pack. Shit. Cancel the dinner reservation.

As promised, there was coffee waiting for me in the kitchen, along with Jon, dressed in sweatpants and an old Otters T-shirt that had seen better days. "I have so much to do," I said.

He shook his head. "Get your gear. I'll pack some stuff up for you. You can come back later to get whatever else you need. You don't have to worry about getting all of it now. Plus, you'll be home—there's probably still a ton of things in your apartment, right?"

There was, yeah. I took the coffee, drank, and looked around. "I really like it here, though."

"I know. Look, we'll figure out the logistics, okay? There's time. I want to make this work, you want to make this work. We're only an hour apart. I mean, there are couples in entirely different cities who make this stuff work."

Jon's coffee tasted perfect. It cut through the rest of the fog in my head and the weight of what Jon was saying finally kicked in. "You want to keep dating. Like—really—want—"

Jon heaved a sigh. "Babe, come here."

The brevity of that made me blink. I shuffled closer. He took the cup from my hands and placed it on the island, then pulled me into a kiss that had me startled, then moaning, then nearly weak in my knees. I planted a hand on the island and wrapped the other around him.

When he relented, he pulled back enough to look me in the eyes. "Yes," he said, emphatically. "I want to keep dating you. If the Lions were in Florida, I'd be calling my agent to get me traded closer to you. This is for real for me. Pretty sure it is for you, too?"

"Oh. Um." I swallowed. "Fuck, yes. I—if there was time..." I glanced at the clock. I really wanted him right then and there.

Jon rolled his eyes, probably feeling my desire against him. He gave me a little shove. "There's no time. Go get your gear. Swing by on the way to Pittsburgh, and I'll have stuff packed for you."

I grabbed the coffee and drank it as quickly as I could while I gathered my wallet, keys, and coat. "Wait, I made reservations..."

"Where and when? I'll handle it."

"You can still go."

He waved a hand. "The birthday will keep. I'll be thirty for 364 more days. Rain check." He paused. "Or in this case, really fucking good news-check."

I laughed at that, feeling lighter. This would work. We would work.

A kiss goodbye, and I was out the door.

I guess the staff at the arena must've gotten word, too, because all of my gear was packed up and waiting for me when I got there. "Good luck, Dragon! Make us proud," Hank said.

Back at Jon's, there was a suitcase and a suit bag waiting for me. "I know you have suits at home, but these are clean and pressed. I also packed the book you were reading, and a couple others. All your toiletries."

"I love you," I said. "I hate leaving, but—I want to play." I was going back to the big show, back to the team I thought didn't want me.

Well, they wanted me now.

"Of course you want to play. Call your mom when you get to Pittsburgh." He helped me load my things into the SUV.

Hell, I'd call her hands-free on the way. "Will you tell everyone at the bar?"

Another kiss, this one lingering. "Of course," he whispered. "I love you, too."

"Happy birthday."

God that smile. The way his dark eyes sparkled in the winter's morning light. "Score me a goal tonight, eh?"

"Absolutely." Hell, I'd score him a hat trick, if I had the chance.

Another peck, and he was shooing me into the SUV, and I was on the road. An hour and ten minutes later, I was pulling into my spot at my apartment.

Surreal. Wonderful. Maddening. Jon wasn't here.

But I was, and I was absolutely determined to prove to the Lions that they hadn't made a mistake calling me back up. I ran my bags up to the apartment, then headed to the arena for morning skate.

WALKING INTO THE LIONS ARENA THIS MORNING HAD been a surreal experience. My badge worked, like always. The staff was familiar, and of course my teammates, but my stall in the locker room had been shifted slightly. In my old stall was Gavin Lacey, the kid they'd called up when I'd been sent down, and my new stall was next to his.

Gavin had done okay so far. Handful of goals. Some nice assists. He was fast on the forecheck, as Jon had said, but was a little hesitant when finishing.

I'd been greeted warmly and loudly by the other guys, including Bearsy, who was still around, rehabbing his ankle. "Glad to be back?" he asked.

"Excited," I said. "Glad for the opportunity." I paused and added, "The Otters are fun though. Really helped me here." I tapped my head.

Bearsy nodded. "Good group of guys down there."

I settled into my new stall and started pulling equipment out of my bag, then turned to my neighbor. "You're Gavin, right?"

He nodded and eyed me. "You're Drake."

"Duck," Bearsy added.

I laughed, because I hadn't heard that in a while. "God, I forgot about that. They were calling me Dragon down there."

"Dragon?" Bearsy said. "Why Dragon?"

"Because it's better than Duck," I replied. "At least, that's what Jonny said."

At the mention of Jon, Gavin cracked a smile. "God, he's the best. How's everyone doing down there, anyway?"

Over the course of the morning, I filled in Gavin (who'd been given the nickname Silky) on how the Otters were doing, and in turn, learned about all I'd missed the past month and a half. Mostly about different line combinations and changes to the power play and penalty kill.

Morning skate wasn't a full one, but I had a feeling I'd be slotting in with the bottom two lines, and maybe on the kill. I still wasn't much of a PKer, but I'd taken some shifts with the Otters PK unit, since Coach Macintosh liked everyone being able to kill penalties. Robinson had me on the PK unit during the morning skate.

"You've been mostly on the top line and on the power play in Greensburg, yeah?" Coach asked.

"Lately, yeah. But I'll play wherever you need me, Coach" I said. "I can do the work."

He nodded. "That's what I like to hear."

After practice, he pulled me aside. "You look good out there, but is there anything new, health-wise we need to know about?"

I started to shake my head, then hesitated. Because sperm-doner was still out there. Coach must've seen because he raised an eyebrow. "It's not exactly health-related," I said. "I had some issues earlier in the season with someone on social media...and my family." I quickly filled him in on what had happened.

He sat back in his chair. "Well shit, Drake. That's pretty heavy stuff. You should've told us."

"I know." I scratched my neck. "I'd thought I'd handled it, but he contacted me again around my birthday."

"You give us the details, and we'll make sure security is up-to-date."

Muscles in my back unlocked. "Thank you, sir."

I caught a nap in my apartment to make up for the lack of sleep. There was a lot adrenaline could do, but nothing really beat having enough rest and recovery under your belt.

When I woke, there was a text from Jon.

> Took care of everything. Have a good game. 🩶

Man. I still felt a little bad about missing out on dinner with him on his birthday. I was so damn lucky he understood. I shot off a quick text back:

> Love you too. Everything's good here.

Then I was into my suit and heading back to the area for tonight's game. Turned out I wasn't on the third or fourth line tonight, but the second—as I had been last year. And on the second unit for the power play. "Can you handle that, kid?"

"You bet, Coach."

My teammates slapped me on the back, and we got situated in the hall to head out onto the ice for warmups. I never really cared where I was in the line, but I loved all the yelling, chest thumping and crazy rituals that went on before we skated out. It was loud and felt like...home. Like I belonged here.

When I burst out onto the ice for warmups, there was a smattering of cheers from the crowd. I took a lap and was shocked to see several signs welcoming me back, either with my name, number, or a picture of a duck.

It wasn't those signs that had me nearly falling over my skates. As it was, I transitioned backward and rammed into the boards close to the goal in shock.

It was a simple sign. Black capital letters written in Sharpie on white cardstock:

DRAGON: PUCK FOR A DINNER DATE?

Holding the sign against the glass was the person I least expected to see here, and he was grinning his thousand-watt smile, eyes twinkling like stars in the bright arena lights.

Jon. Jonny *fucking* Eriksson.

Gavin skated up next to me in the corner and stick handled a puck. "Dragon, huh?" He was smiling.

"I'm going to kill him," I muttered, then grabbed an errant puck and tossed it over the glass to Jon, who deftly caught it. Somehow, his toothy grin widened, which I didn't think was possible. I gave the glass a fist bump, then got back to warming up, my face more than a little warm under my helmet.

I hoped my visor wouldn't fog up.

The looks my teammates gave me varied from confused to amused. Luckily, there was no anger. Then again, Brodie and a couple others wouldn't have stood for it.

When we got back to the locker room after warmups, it was Brodie (who was wearing an A tonight) who put his hands on his hips and gave me a look. "Got something you want to tell us, *Dragon?*" He was smiling almost as brightly as Jon had been.

Well, there was no sense in beating around the bush. "Uh, I'm dating Jon Eriksson?"

That got me a bunch of cheers and pats on the back.

"Damn," Brodie said. "He's a looker."

Gavin laughed. "I've never actually seen him that happy before."

I whirled around. "What? He's always happy! It's his natural state of being!"

That had Dimitri Vasileiou, our backup goalie, snorting. "No, no, Silky's right. Jonny's happy, sure, but that?" He shook his head. "What did you do to him?"

"Whoa, whoa," Cutts said. "Don't need the details."

I covered my face with my hands. "I'm really gonna kill him."

Coach Robinson shook his head. "Gotta fucking send Mac a bottle of scotch." He cleared his throat to get our attention. "If you boys are done? You've got a game to play against a pretty tough opponent..."

I was grateful for the shift in the spotlight, though I did get a few "Hey, congrats" comments before we headed back out onto the ice. After that, everything was a focused whirl of action.

Coach wasn't kidding about this being a hard match. The other team, the Buffalo Jets, were feisty tonight. Hard hitting. But they were also playing very tight, and our forecheck wasn't getting much behind their D, even if we were the slightly faster team. They scored first during the first period. Early in the second, while defending our zone, the puck bounced off Chester's goalie pads straight to me. One of their D was out of position, so I saw the breakout clearly. Evidently, my linemates did, too. I went flying up the ice, on what turned out to be a two on zip. I looked to Z, one of our big wingers, the entire time we skated up, faked a pass, then sent the puck zipping past the overcommitted goalie, into the back of the net.

Goal lights. Horn. Cheering crowd, and then my teammates crushed me. "Atta boy, Dragon!" Z said.

Felt so good. Like last year—or this year on the Otters. No more heavy weight. No more thinking I was as useless as my sperm-donor had said.

I'd gotten a goal for my team. Just like I'd promised Jon.

After fist-bumps, when I took my seat on the bench, Brodie slapped me on the back. "Got the magic back."

Was it magic? I didn't know. Hockey was luck and skill and mood, seemed like. I was glad to be riding the top of the wave again. I was sure I'd have my slumps. As long as I remembered why I was here, it'd be fine. I had the love of the game to pull me through.

We ended up winning in overtime on a goal from Gavin, who Coach had put out with me and Z. He'd seen a hole, and we'd rushed into the zone and completed a little tic-tac-toe play that had the goalie and the other team's players all scrambled up.

The crowd screamed, our teammates piled onto us in the corner, and the horn blared an extra-long time. We were loud and rambunctious as we headed back into the locker room. Bearsy was there in a suit, giving fist-bumps, and next to him, grinning like the devil, was Jon, all dark hair and mischief, wrapped up in an Otters hoodie, an all-access badge around his neck.

I planted my hand on his chest and gave him a playful shove as I passed. His laughter was joyous.

"You deserved that, Jonny," someone said.

Then we were stripping off gear and Coach was congratulating us on a game well-played. The VIP object—an old helmet with a lion's mane and ears—went to Gavin for his OT goal.

Then they let the press in to talk to us.

I wasn't surprised when a scrum formed around my stall. I answered a bunch of questions about what it was like to be back (great), and how playing with the Otters impacted my game.

I paused and thought about that. "I'm not sure it changed the mechanics of my play," I said. "I was in a bad space when I went down, and the guys there—they helped me find what I'd been missing. The passion for being on the ice. The joy. I play this game because I love it. I needed to remember that."

After everyone cleared out, they let the partners, spouses, and kids in as we filtered out to the lounge to eat our post-game snack, or to do a short workout in the gym. It was then that Jon reappeared, and we headed into the lounge together.

"Jonnieeee!" Bearsy said. "Taking up with the Dragon."

Jon scratched the back of his head. "Dragon is so much better than Duck. What the hell were you thinking with that nickname, man?"

Gavin laughed. "They're calling me Silky."

"It's because you're so smooooth." Bearsy said.

Jon rolled his eyes. "Silky? As in Lacey and Silky? My God, I thought I taught you better than that, Kev."

"Better than my juniors nickname," Gavin said.

I bumped Gavin's shoulder. "What was that?"

He made a face. "Panties."

Bearsy gestured at Gavin. "See? Silky's fine. You guys probably called him something like Quilt."

"It was Gabe," Gavin said. "Short for Gabriel."

"He came as an angel for Halloween," Jon supplied.

I just laughed.

Jon plopped himself down on the other side of me. "Hey. Thanks for the puck."

"No problem. I expect a dinner date." I paused. "Finally."

"Eh, we keep having issues with those, but I'll see what I can do."

Gavin butted in. "Wait, you two haven't been on a *date* yet? But you're dating?" He raised an eyebrow at Jon. "I heard about your rules."

"Not an 'official' date," Jon said, with air-quotes. "But we got to know each other pretty well before we—" He waved his hand.

I put an arm around Jon. "He broke his rules for me."

"The universe conspired against dinner dates," Jon countered. "Case in point, tonight. My birthday dinner."

"Shit, Jonny, it's your birthday?" Bearsy said. "Happy birthday!"

That had a bunch of the players, spouses, partners, employees—basically anyone in the lounge—singing happy birthday to Jon while Gavin went on a mission to find something that would count as cake.

That ended up being an orange cranberry muffin from this morning. Gavin even found a candle to stick into it, and that prompted another round of singing so Jon could blow it out.

Everything was perfect. Being here with the Lions. Jon rolling his eyes but smiling so brightly as he tucked into the muffin. The kids running around the lounge.

Yeah. I belonged here—but so did Jon.

Coach pulled me away to fill me in on the upcoming

schedule, and when I got back, Jon was talking to a couple of the partners and spouses.

I curled an arm around his waist. "Can I steal the birthday boy away?"

That got me some laughs, but no objections. When we were free from other people, I bumped my hip against Jon's. "Come home with me?"

"Absolutely," he said. "Please."

"Make your birthday even happier?"

"I don't think you can," he said. "It's been pretty fantastic, actually. Got to see my boyfriend score a goal in his first game back in the big league."

If that wasn't ever a challenge to make it better. "Come on, let's go."

We headed to the parking garage, arms around each other's waists.

CHAPTER 12

JON

I'd expected Drake's apartment to be one of those small one-bedroom loft things. It wasn't that at all. He had three bedrooms on the top two floors of a building downtown that had been renovated and converted from offices or storage or something. The exterior walls were brick, the floors old wood, and everything had a clean look to it. Stainless steel appliances. Lots of reds and yellows, with hints of blues. It probably looked spectacular in the sunlight, given the big windows.

I didn't get much of a tour. Instead, he pressed me up against the island in the kitchen and kissed me insistently. Between sharp nips, he muttered, "Thank you. For coming to my game."

"Beat watching it on TV. You were only an hour away, and it's easy enough to get a last-minute ticket, so here I am."

He pulled back, and fingered the access badge I still had around my neck. "And this?"

"Oh, that? Someone from PR texted me during the game and asked me where I was. They came and gave this to me. Also told me where the spouses and partners usually sit and that I should call them next time I need a ticket." I tugged him closer for another kiss.

"Wait, they saw you, somehow? Knew you were there?"

Oh. I felt my face heat. "Uh, you haven't checked social media, have you? Because, yeah. Everyone knows I was there, *now*."

There was a cute look of absolute panic on his face, then he whipped out his phone. "Where?"

"Instagram."

I knew what he'd find, since he'd been tagged in the photo, too. One of the photographers at the game had caught the moment when he'd tossed the puck to me, and there we were, both laughing with the sign I'd made. Those things got uploaded to a site, and the team pretty much had access to all the photos as the game went on, so of course they'd posted a comment:

An Otter and a Dragon??

The comments had blown up under that. Most of them were nice, or cute. Some were homophobic, because some people were awful. But everyone now knew there was something between us.

"Wow," Drake said. "Guess we're out, huh?" Then he placed his phone upside down on the kitchen island and tugged me away. "Let me give you the tour of my bedroom."

I let him pull me through the living room to the stairs. "Am I going to see any of it, or is 'bedroom tour' a euphemism for 'face into the mattress?'"

His grin was wicked, and I shivered in delight.

I did catch a tiny glimpse of his bedroom (another brick wall, some kind of painting of a beach, and light-colored furniture) before we were making out again, and his hands were tugging at the hem of my sweatshirt. "Get these clothes off so I can show you my bedspread."

Didn't take long to strip, and before I knew it, I was on my hands and knees on said bedspread. Not that I noticed much, not with Drake stroking my cock and tonguing my hole. It was all I could do to have any coherent thoughts. I curled my fingers into the cloth and moaned his name. "Gonna make me come like that."

"Nuh uh." He gave my ass a soft slap and fondled my balls. "I want my dick nice and deep inside you when you do. Want your ass milking every last drop out of me."

I bit my lip and shuddered because oh my God, imagining that had me about to shoot my load. "Better make it soon."

Of course, he took his time. I was beginning to think he had an edging kink—or he just liked to hear me beg and whine and beg some more, because he had me babbling and pleading for him to fuck me already for what felt like an hour. I could barely hold myself up on my elbows, and my throat was raw from moaning.

"I love the way you sound. The way you look," he said. "All strung out. Because of me. For me. You're so damn beautiful, and I get to turn you into *this* whenever you want."

"*Please*, Drake."

"Patience."

"Don't have any. You've used it all up. I'm the most—" He slid two fingers inside me. "Oh God."

"There you go."

He didn't need to finger-fuck me. Hell, he probably didn't need much lube. I was more than ready for him. I'd have told him that, if I could've produced more than grunts and whimpers.

"Fucking perfect," he said.

So was his dick finally pressing into me and his grip on my hips as he drove himself deeper and faster inside until we—and the bed—were rocking with every thrust. Felt so damn good. "Best birthday," I whispered.

Drake answered by thrusting deep and holding himself there. "I want to do this every year. Fuck you at the beginning and at the end."

I squirmed around him, wanting more of him, wanting this to never end—but needing so desperately to come. "*Please!*"

He gave me what I asked for, moving again, hard and with purpose while I worked my cock.

"Yeah, that's it, Jon. You're so fucking tight. Come on—do it. Come for me."

I did, with a moan that was mostly breath. Jizz coated my fingers and his bedspread while he pounded into me, hitting me just right to keep the pleasure going and going.

"Fuck," he moaned. "Oh God." Then he was burying himself as deep as he could, and we collapsed together onto his bed.

After we caught our breath, he whispered in my ear, "How'd you like the bedroom tour?"

I huffed. "It's a lovely bedspread. Let's visit it more often."

He vibrated with laughter.

OVER THE NEXT COUPLE WEEKS, DRAKE AND I GOT INTO a routine of seeing each other when our schedules aligned, which was more often than I'd thought it might be. Yes, there were road trips that took one or the other or both of us out of town, but there were also days off, or non-game days when we got together. Sometimes, I'd drive to Pittsburgh and hang out with the Lions partners and spouses while watching Drake play. Several times, Drake came to Greensburg to watch me and the Otters. He got to know Ebba pretty well.

Hell, he dragged some of the bar patrons to games, too. Or maybe they took him—hard to tell. I do know that he managed to make it to the Otters Pride game, and the pool queens took it upon themselves to dress him for the occasion.

Those legs in fishnets? Oh my God, that would live in the fantasy file in my mental filing cabinet for a long time. And yes, I saved a whole bunch of photos.

The best part, though, was that we finally had our dinner date. And it was absolutely uneventful.

One of his days off coincided with a non-game day for me, so after practice, I drove to his apartment. We'd ended up playing tourist in town—going shopping in the Strip District, then checking out the Warhol Museum before ultimately having dinner at one of the various restaurants in the city. This one, an Argentinean grill, was down the street from his place. Drake had snagged a reservation earlier in the day, and miracle of miracles, there were no crises, no phone calls, no asteroids falling out of the sky and obliterating the East Coast. Nothing. We walked into the place, got seated upstairs, and had a great meal.

"So," he said, leaning back and gesturing around him. "This count as a date?"

"This is most definitely a date," I said. "Want to split dessert?"

After we ate that, he came over, sat on my lap, and we

took several couples selfies, including one of him kissing me on the cheek. Those went onto Instagram.

An actual date. Had only taken a couple months.

Whenever he came to my place, the cats mobbed him. Come to think of it, whenever he came to the bar, the regulars mobbed him, too. I didn't blame anyone—Drake was spectacular and fun to be with, now that he'd found his game.

His scoring touch was certainly back. On the Lions he was maintaining more than a point per game pace since his return. Lots of stories in the press about him rekindling his love of the game with the Otters, and he'd even penned a thank-you note to the fans in Greensburg.

I didn't mind sharing him with fans—he was pretty much recognized anywhere we went in Pittsburgh, and more people were talking about me, albeit as Gunner Eriksson's kid or Drake's boyfriend. Or both.

During the All-Star break, I was very grateful we were able to steal away down to Sanibel Island. Neither of us had made our respective league's team, mostly because that decision had been made for the NAPH during Drake's slump.

He didn't care. A long weekend at the beach, in the warm and sun went a long way to chasing away the wintertime blues, and it was just nice to spend time with each other that didn't involve hockey. We ate, swam, relaxed, and read to each other. Honestly, couples goals, I guess.

I kind of kept waiting for the other shoe to drop—you hear so much about a relationship's honeymoon period, before the friction sets in and you start squabbling at each other or something—but that didn't happen.

"Did you and Papa ever fight when you were dating," I asked my mother one afternoon in March.

Her tone turned concerned. "Are you and Drake having problems?"

"No. Everything's fine. We're good and happy. I think I'm more in love with him every time we see each other. I'm trying to figure out if that's normal—there's no handbook to look this stuff up in, and I've never been here before. Does that feeling...ever stop?"

She'd laughed at that. "If you're asking me if I still look at your father and feel wonder that this man is with me, of all people—I do. If you're asking me if we ever have our differences—well, you know we do. Not often, but you've seen us disagree."

I had. Didn't happen often, but sometimes they'd get into intense discussions about something and be on opposite sides. "I don't know if I'd call that fighting, though..."

"Jon, the most important things in a relationship are love and communication. If you and Drake have that, none of your disagreements will seem like fights, either."

Maybe that was true. Everything was so good and this felt sustainable. Drake was happy. I was happy. What more did we need?

The future would take care of itself, I supposed.

THIS GAME. THIS *FUCKING* GAME. I PUNCHED THE TOP of the boards in front of me at the bench, and for once was glad Drake wasn't here to watch me play. We'd been winning three-two when the other team had pulled their goalie and managed to tie things up with a minute-three to go.

We were *this close* to snapping our four-game losing streak. And now, not only did we have to hold on to prevent them from scoring again, the game was likely going into overtime. Which we hadn't been all that great at, lately.

I knew seasons had their ups and downs, but I was getting pretty damn tired of this set of downs. The Otters were better than this current slump. A lot of fans said that we were missing our Dragon, and yeah, we could've used him, but even without Drake on the ice, we'd been winning games. Alfie had really stepped up, scoring seemingly every game.

But the past week and a half—all our luck had dried up.

Well, not all. As the seconds counted down, we did well to keep the puck out of our end. Even got some really good scoring chances—but no dice on a goal.

Well, overtime it was, then.

Mac and his assistants huddled us during the break while the ice crew shoveled snow off the ice. The first three out were Lou, Hardy, and Bike. They won the faceoff and got into the offensive zone. Even got a few shots off before the other team stole the puck. They didn't get much time in our end, though, before we reclaimed it.

Our shift changes were good, and after another three guys went out, it was my turn, along with Bruda and Alfie. A little bit of a risk going with three forwards, but I guess Mac trusted how I saw the ice. Hopefully that confidence wouldn't come back to bite us.

For a while, there were no chances. The other team's guys had been out longer, and as we circled, I saw one of their guys hedging toward the benches. I think Alfie figured it out, too, because he dropped back while I crept forward. The instant their guy headed off, Alfie had the puck to me, and I was heading toward their goalie, as fast as I could go. My wheels had never been that great, but they were good enough that I deked their defenseman, faked a forehand shot, and backhanded the puck bar down into the net.

I pumped my arms up in celebration—and then I was upended. Tripped. Stick, foot, I don't know how. All I knew was that time hung still, and I realized just how off-balance I was and how close the boards were. Fuck. Fuck!

Then everything happened in an instant. The impact. The pain. The shock. I was on my back on the ice. The goal horn was going off, the crowd was screaming, and Alfie looked scared shitless. Pale.

"Jon? Jonny? Hey no, don't move."

Fuck. Oh God. My arm. There was something very wrong with my arm. A sickly feeling grew in my body, and I knew tears were pricking at my eyes. Above me, Cal, our athletic trainer, appeared. "Jonny, you okay?"

"No." My voice felt far away. "Arm."

"Do you need a stretcher?"

Fuck, no. This was bad enough. "I think I can get up."

It hurt like hell, even not using my right arm, but I got myself onto my knees, then feet, and was able to skate off. (Of course it was my dominant arm. Goddamn it.)

After that—well—stuff got blurry. Mostly because everything fucking hurt. The team doctor and the arena EMTs met me and hauled me into the medical room. We managed to get my gear off, and they gave me a battery of commands. My fingers still worked, so that was good, but I didn't want to move my arm at all, and the pain was creeping up my neck. "There's something really wrong," I kept saying, and they made noises about sending me to the hospital and some other chatter. They did end up getting a catheter into my good arm. "Hey, we're going to get you some fluids and something for the pain, okay?"

That sounded great. Because I kind of wanted to chop my bad arm off.

Somewhere along the line, Mac appeared. "We've contacted your father—"

"Oh God, no—"

"Shut up, Jonny. He's your contact, so we contacted him."

Fuck. "Don't tell Drake. He'll worry and—"

"Yeah, because him learning from the press during his after-game media scrum is the best way for him to find out."

Okay, no, that was worse. I twisted my face.

"They'll let him know. You're on your way to Pittsburgh, anyway."

What? "Why?"

"Because," our doctor chimed in, "your shoulder is broken. You'll likely need surgery, and the facilities there are some of the best in the world."

Right. Right. The pain wasn't receding like I thought, but I kind of didn't care anymore. "Great. Can you turn my brain off?"

He gave a half-chuckle, did something with the tube running to my arm, my vision went wonky, and then I was gone.

CHAPTER 13

DRAKE

Third period. We were down by one coming out of the intermission and the only thing on our minds was winning this game against New Jersey. They weren't even that strong of a team, but for some reason the Lions couldn't beat them at home, going back several seasons. Call it a curse or bad luck or whatever. In my mind, it was more of a self-fulfilling prophecy, since we got antsy and gripped our sticks too tight—all the cliches about bad play. So of course Brodie blocked a shot with his foot and left the game at the end of last period. Wasn't broken, but he'd bruised it bad enough that he wasn't coming back out for the third. No sense in those kind of heroics before the playoffs—we'd need them during.

But that left me centering the top line. No pressure, right? Coach said he'd seen film of me with the Otters, and he had no doubts. Bearsy had no doubts.

I had doubts, sure, but also aspirations. I wanted to be the one who lifted the "curse" on the team by changing attitudes and getting us believing we could win. It was what Jon would've done in the same situation.

"Look," I said, "we can do this. Their goalie isn't some sort of acrobatic wall. He's bobbled pucks. Left the net wide open. Puck bounces the other direction, and we'd be up five to two."

"So what do we do?" Gavin asked.

"Don't miss the net," Brodie, said from where he was sitting with a cold pack on his foot, "unlike me."

I laughed at that. "Yeah, I mean, that one's obvious, but honestly, just keep peppering him with shots. Stop reacting, start acting. Their D isn't *that* good. We have to be more aggressive on the forecheck, like when you guys played Seattle."

"You watched that?" Gavin said.

"Yup." I paused, then added, "Watched a bunch of NAPH games once I got over myself." I missed watching games with Jon. He was like an extra coach, pointing out both the good and bad of plays. It'd helped me to see plays from a different point of view and to understand that even the best fucked up.

"Anyway, if there's actually some kind of curse on the team, then nothing we do should work, right? So let's have fun, force them to play hard, and see what happens?"

What happened was a turnaround. No idea if it was what I'd said that caused the momentum shift or that flukey goal from our defensemen, Cal, that tied us up under two minutes into the third. Nothing special to Cal's shot. Simply a blast from the point that hit one of their players and then floated past the goalie in what seemed like slow motion.

With the game tied, suddenly, our bench was hyped, and their goalie was... not. The next goal was mine, and at first people didn't know how I'd gotten it in.

I'd simply noticed the goalie's reverse VH stance was off

and he'd left a hole against the post by his foot, so when the puck bounced to me at the side of the net, I jammed it home as hard as I could, and it went in.

Garbage goal. But who cared? We were up by one.

In the end, my goal stood as the game winner. We added two more and beat them five-two, finally breaking the curse.

Nothing was going to topple me off of this high. We were hollering and shouting as we made it to the locker room. Our winning song was blaring, and everyone was smacking me, congratulating me for the game winner. I even got the Lion helmet as game MVP.

Then Will, one of the trainers, came over and touched my shoulder. "Coach wants to see you."

My stomach dropped to my feet. It went through the floor when I caught the expression on the trainer's face.

Oh fuck. What'd happened? Was it something I'd done? Was my mom okay? Had that asshole sperm donor contacted the team? Every single possibility ramped through my head. I stripped off the rest of my gear. Bearsy shoved a protein bar and water into my hands. "You're shaking."

No shit. The look Coach gave me when I entered the video room didn't help. He did pat the air with his hands. "Don't panic. Everyone's fine." Then he grimaced. "Mostly."

"Just—tell me."

He nodded. "We wanted to get to you before the reporters did so you aren't blindsided. Jonny Eriksson took a bad fall into the boards. Broke his shoulder. He needs surgery, so he's on his way here."

Oh shit. I sank into a nearby chair. "What happened?"

Coach huffed. "He made the play of his life, won the

game in overtime, then got tripped up. Just bad luck. He skated off on his own power. Isn't concussed. Just a broken shoulder."

"Fuck." Jon was hurt and I wasn't there. I set the water and protein bar on the floor and dropped my head into my hands. I had no idea what went into shoulder surgery, but I knew even minor stuff to shoulders sucked hard and was painful to work through in PT.

"He's going to be okay," Coach said.

I looked up and studied Coach. "What aren't you telling me?"

He shook his head. "You'll see on the replay. But be thankful it was his shoulder that took the impact."

I knew the unspoken thoughts. Be thankful it wasn't his head. Or neck. I shuddered. Yeah, I was going to watch the replay. But not yet. Because Jon was *hurt* and I wasn't *there* with him. "Which hospital?"

Coach rattled off the name of a hospital in the Oakland neighborhood of Pittsburgh. "Look, shower and eat something before taking off."

I picked up the protein bar and shook it.

"More than that, Williams."

"I know." Fuck, Fuck. I needed to be there. But Coach was right. And Jon would be exasperated if I showed up not having eaten, and then... probably call a nurse to try to order me food or something. "Thanks," I said to Coach, "for pulling me away before the media got in."

"You didn't need that. Neither does Jonny. He's a good man. So are you. Now get out of here, get the stink off you, and get some calories. Then get to him."

So that's what I did, as fast as I could. When I retrieved my phone, I found messages from Jon.

> Hey, I'm fine. Don't worry about me. It's not as bad as it looks on TV. I mean, I need surgery, but it's fine. I called my parents, and Papa is coming out, so don't worry, please.

> Oh! Great goal tonight! GWG! Keep finding those holes in the goalies.

> But seriously. I'm fine. Please don't run over here if you have other things you need to do.

I reread the messages as I walked to my SUV and rolled my eyes.

> Well, I'm on my way to the hospital. Tell them I'm allowed to see you.

I was sure visiting hours were over, but this was Jon and I was me. There were privileges to being a sports star. Before I got to my SUV, I had a reply.

> Already did. 🤍

Of course he had. This was a man who saw five moves ahead on the ice. He didn't want to inconvenience me, but he also knew I'd come, despite his protests. Something in my body loosened, and I let out a long breath. God, I loved him so much. I ached in my soul, but I pushed that aside. I'd deal with my feelings later. Right now was about Jon.

Didn't actually take that long to get to the hospital from downtown—I'd forgotten how close it really was. Maybe not blocks away, but within fifteen minutes I was walking to his room. "He may be out of it," the nurse at the station had said. "He's on pain medication."

When I got to Jon's room, he was scrolling through his phone, his brows deeply furrowed, as if he didn't understand what he was looking at. I paused at the door. "Hey."

He beamed at me with a loopy smile. "Baby, hi! You're here! You didn't need to come." He grimaced a little and dropped the phone onto his bed. "My arm's broken," he whined. "I can't do anything. I fucking hate it." He sighed dramatically. "But I'm glad you're here. You didn't have to, but I'm happy." Another pause. "Well no, not happy. This sucks. But you're here."

Yup. Definitely on painkillers. "Yeah, I'm here." I entered, found the guest chair and pulled it up next to his bed. "Thought your shoulder was broken?"

He waved with his left hand. "Yeah, yeah. Shoulder. Arm. Whatever. I can't use it and it hurts. I don't care that it hurts, but it still hurts. This stuff is okay, though." He flailed his good arm with the attached tubing. "So much better than when I cared that it hurt."

"Uh huh." I took his left hand in mine. "Guess they'll do surgery in the morning?"

That furrow again, and boy were his eyes glassy. "I think so. Said I should sleep."

"Probably should." That's when I spotted what he'd been scrolling through on his phone. Hotels. "Hey babe, what are you doing?" I picked the phone up.

"Ugh. Trying to find a decent place I can live in with the cats. After the surgery. Not going to be able to drive, and they want me close to here for doctors and PT and all that. Papa said he'd come live with me but—" He gestured at the phone. "Thor and Loki. Maybe I'll buy a place or something."

That...was the first time I'd ever heard Jon say anything to indicate how wealthy he must be. We'd never really discussed finances other than his comments early on, and he'd been fine with me paying my fair share. The idea he could just buy a place... At least two bedrooms, one for him and one for his father. Well.

Then again, his papa was Gunner Eriksson.

Of course he was planning ahead, but the drugs were making him more than a little dopey, because the solution to this problem was obvious. "I don't think you should be worrying about that right now. Or, you know, spending any money while on painkillers."

"Ugh, probably. But they're all alone there." Some neurons must have fired correctly through the drug haze, because he brightened and met my gaze. "Hey! You can check on them." Then his face fell "Unless you have a road trip. Oh God, you probably have a road trip. I'm sorry, I didn't want you to worry or—"

I squeezed his hand. "Babe, I'll go get the cats tomorrow. They can stay with me. You and your father can stay with me. I've got three bedrooms, remember?"

"But road trips?"

"Five game homestand," I said. "You'll be recovering and your dad will be here while I'm gone."

He furrowed his brow again. "Yeah," he said slowly, then nodded. "Yeah, that'll work. I should've thought of that."

"Well, drugs." I gave him a smile. "You're out of it."

"Probably." He closed his eyes and laid his head back against the pillows. "God, I'm tired. I hate this. I'm glad you came. You fixed everything. I love you."

I leaned over him to press a kiss to his forehead. "Love you too. Don't worry about anything. Sleep. Do you want me to stay overnight?"

"No. I mean, yes, but no. I'd feel too guilty and probably

wouldn't sleep. Feel better if I knew you could get a good night's rest. You won your game. You should rest."

"You won your game, too."

He huffed a laugh. "I get surgery as a prize!"

"Yeah. That sucks." I rose and kissed his forehead again. "Babe, try to sleep. Do what the docs say. I'll be back tomorrow."

"Mmm," Jon muttered before he closed his eyes.

I left him to sleep, thanked the nurses on my way out, and headed back to my apartment. I'd have to rearrange my office and get a bed, but that wasn't a concern. The place was big enough, and I'd feel better if Jon and his dad were somewhere that wasn't a soul-sucking hotel. Returning the favor, as it were.

Despite all that was running through my head, I fell asleep hard and woke early. After texting with the team, I found out when Jon's surgery was (nine this morning) and that Coach was giving me a maintenance day. So a coffee and an hour drive later, and I was letting myself into Jon's house.

Loki practically tackled me, so I swept his big fluffy butt up into my arms. "Hey, it's okay! I know you've been alone forever!"

Meanwhile Thor meowed forlornly at my feet. "You guys are going on a trip, okay? Going to come live with me for a bit."

I set Loki on the floor and quieted his protests by feeding both him and Thor. Then I stood in the living room with my hands on my hips, making a mental checklist of what I'd need. Thank goodness I'd lived here for a while, because I knew where everything was. Took me the better part of the morning to pack the cats' stuff up. The smaller of the two scratching posts fit in my SUV, thankfully.

I also grabbed a bunch of clothing, the pile of books by Jon's bed, his laptop, all his chargers, and the perishable stuff in the fridge (that went into a cooler he kept in the garage).

Wrangling the cats into their carriers wasn't as hard as I thought it would be, and I didn't even lose any blood in the process. Loki complained bitterly, which set Thor to whining, too, but I'd take that over having them here on their own.

The ride back was another hour, but this time with a chorus of unhappy cat noises, which I tried to quell by singing nonsense songs to them like Jon did. I think everyone in the SUV was quite happy when I reached my apartment. Cats went up first, and they vanished up the stairs to the floor with the bedrooms as soon as I let them out of the carriers.

Probably thought I was catnapping them, or something.

Spent a few more hours setting things up in the house, and the cats came out of hiding. Loki bumped up against my legs and let me pick him up. "Your dad's hurt. He's gonna spend some time here, so you guys need to be here too, okay?"

Loki meowed at me and looked unimpressed, but clung to me when I attempted to place him on the floor, so I ended up carrying twenty-some pounds of cat around the house with me.

Guess I was getting my off-ice workout after all.

When my phone chimed, I maneuvered Loki into one arm and snatched it up to see a text from our GM telling me Jon was out of surgery and that everything went well. I let out a breath.

I wasn't worried, per se, but hearing that Jon was okay felt like a weight lifted off me.

I deposited Loki on the scratching post. "Sorry, bud. Gotta go see your dad." I grabbed Jon's phone charger and the book he'd been reading, and headed out.

Jon wasn't the only person in his room when I got there. The man sitting at his bedside and speaking quietly with Jon in Swedish was utterly recognizable. Jon's father noticed me first, and his smile was almost a twin to the one Jon had so often. "Ah," he said. "Your young man is here."

Jon's smile was a tired version of his father's. "Hey. You're here."

"I am. And I brought your phone charger and the book you were reading."

As I entered the room, his father stood, and I was reminded that Gunner Eriksson, at six foot four, was taller than his son. Taller than me. His blond hair had silvered over the years, and his clean-shaven face had mischievous wrinkles. His smile, and the twinkling in his blue eyes were so akin to Jon's that I wondered how in the world I'd missed that these two were related when I'd met Jon all those months ago.

I gave Jon his charger and book, and leaned in for a quick kiss. Jon looked so much better. Tired, yes. Very rumpled. His arm and shoulder were in a high tech–looking sling, but gone was the glassy-eyed stare of the night before.

Jon's father cleared his throat. "You must be Drake. It's a pleasure to meet you, finally."

I shook his hand. "Hello, sir. It's nice to meet you, too. Even if it's because—"

"I broke myself," Jon said.

His father sighed. "Jon, you were tripped."

"And broke myself," Jon replied, cheerily.

"Anyway," I said, because I knew Jon would go off on

that tangent if I let him, "Wish it had been for better circumstances."

"Same. And *please*. Gunner or Erik. Sir is too formal, and I am not particularly that."

"Gunner." I grabbed a folding chair I'd spotted in the corner and took a seat on the other side of Jon's bed. "Loki and Thor are settling into the apartment. Loki wouldn't let me set him down for a while."

Jon rolled his eyes. "Oh, that big baby. Thanks for getting them." He tapped the book. "And this." He paused. "And for keeping me from drunk-buying a place last night."

Gunner laughed at that. "You didn't!" He turned to me. "He didn't, did he?"

"Well, he was thinking about it. But I have three bedrooms. Enough for the cats and you two, I think."

Gunner chuckled at that. "Loki does take up a lot of space. And Thor tries." He shook his head. "Also, you kids don't need me hanging around. I'll be fine at the William Penn for a week or two."

I was going to protest, but Jon patted my hand. "Don't bother. I tried. Papa enjoys high-end hotels, and this way, we don't have to figure out your office."

Of course, now that Jon's mind was clear, he'd have thought it all through. "It's no problem, though."

Gunner clicked his tongue. "Believe me, I was young once. You two need the space." He held up a hand to stop me from saying anything. "And I've checked your schedule, you don't have any long road trips for another three weeks. Everything is fly in and out. After that, we'll figure things out."

"All right." I recognized where Jon got his stubborn streak from.

"Besides," Jon said, "The other PASOs said they'd take care of me while you're gone."

I blinked. "*Other* PASOs?" That was the first time I'd heard him refer to himself as one of the Lions' partners and significant others, even if he did hang out with the group a lot.

He shrugged, then grimaced. "Shit, I gotta stop doing that. Ugh." Jon shook his head while his father snorted.

"Technically," Gunner said, "He's your significant other. Absolutely not surprised the group here reached out to him. You're well-loved. He's well-loved. With the Lions and the Otters."

"Wait," Jon said. "How do you know this?"

Gunner sat back and gave Jon a look that was so Jon-like that I had to slap my hand over my mouth to keep from roaring in laughter. Jon pinned that same look on me, and I failed to keep the laughter in.

Soon we were all laughing, but Jon waved us to stop. "Shit, it hurts. Fuck." There were tears in his eyes. "I mean, it feels good, because damn, I hate everything about this, and I'm so happy you're both here, but Papa, have you been *spying on me?*"

"No." That was said with every ounce of Eriksson indignation, and Gunner's accent only heightened the impact. "I would never. But word gets back, Jon." He smiled sweetly. "I'm so proud of you. Your team. Your bar. The life you've built." He gestured at me. "The man you've met and chosen."

Jon wiped his eyes. "Stop."

Gunner chuckled, then turned to me. "And you. You took a stumble, then responded the right way, and look at you now. Your name's in all the outlets."

"If it hadn't been for Jon—" I started.

"Stop," Jon said again. "You did the work. I just got you to breathe a little."

"Is that what the kids are calling it these days?"

"Papa!" Jon said, aghast.

Gunner cackled like... well like Jon often did.

"Oh my God," I muttered. "There are two of you."

"Wait until you meet Sofia," Gunner said. "My wife says we three are peas in a pod."

That was a sobering thought. Because—I wanted to meet Jon's sister. I wanted to meet Jon's mother—wanted my mother to meet them, too.

My future was right there, beleaguered and in a sling in a hospital bed. I wanted him *home*, wherever that would end up being.

"I love you," I said.

Jon rubbed his eyes more. "Love you, too. Get me out of here."

Gunner rose. "I'll go see if I can find a nurse or a doctor who can tell us what's next."

When he'd left the room, I leaned in for another kiss. "You're just like your dad."

"I am not. My dad is a Hall of Fame Player. I'm—"

"A good, kind, wonderful man. Just like your dad." I took his hand. "You know we're going to get married, right?"

He barked a laugh. "Yeah. Figured that out a while ago. But I didn't want to scare you with proposing at some weird moment."

"Like in a hospital?"

He gave me a gentle shove. "Exactly."

Eventually, Gunner came back, and after a while, Jon's doctor showed up and we got the schedule for his release and what needed to happen next, and a whole list of post-op items, including a visiting nurse who'd check up on him.

Medications. You named it. Jon was exhausted by the end. "Fucking anesthesia. I always feel like I'm missing half my brain afterward."

"How'd we notice?" I quipped, and he gave me another shove.

"Just for that," Jon said, "can you go get me a coffee? A real one? There's a coffee shop on the first floor."

"God, yes," I said. "Could use one, too. Gunner?"

"If you don't mind, may I come along?"

And that's how I ended up in an elevator with a living hockey legend. Whose son I was going to marry. I didn't know what to say.

Gunner seemed tired but amused. "I took a red-eye to get here. I have no idea the time, except that I want to sleep, but can't. Coffee will help." His gaze met mine. "You've been so good for him. I'm very grateful for that."

"I—" I shook my head. "Truth is, he's been good for me. This is—I owe him this. I love him. This is a small thing."

Gunner nodded. "Believe me, I understand that."

That was a scary thought, because I wasn't sure I did. We collected our coffees and headed back up to Jon's room.

I'd like to say that soon after, we were able to take Jon to my place, but it took several more hours for him to be released, and it was past dinner time when we finally got back to the apartment that contained two very confused cats. They were as happy to see Jon as he was to see them, and he ended up in the living room talking to his father while Loki and Thor sat on him. I ordered takeout from a local Thai restaurant, and we eventually ate.

A yawning Gunner headed back to his hotel, leaving me with Jon and the cats. I joined him on the couch.

"Thank you," Jon said. "So much. For everything. The cats. My laptop and clothing. Even the food you rescued."

He rubbed his head. "It's a lot. Right after a game. Right before another."

"You'd do exactly the same for me."

"I would." We met each other's gazes, and I wrapped an arm—carefully—around him. "You should rest."

"Drake?" Jon's voice sounded small.

"Yeah, babe?"

"Don't make me sleep in the guest room alone. I know maybe I should, but I've missed you, and I feel awful, and I just—"

"Of course." I wasn't going to argue with him. "I'll try not to roll around too much."

Jon snorted. "Gone for a couple months, and you've forgotten that Loki and Thor are going to sandwich you in place."

I helped Jon clean himself up, got his ice bath machine running, and once that was done, we crawled into bed. The cats followed, and yes, they sandwiched me in place.

"I love you, Drake Williams," Jon said. "I fully intend to marry you and have lots of dinner dates for the rest of our lives."

I knew it wasn't the pain meds talking.

"I want that," I said. "Whenever you're ready."

He laughed. "Oh God. Such pressure."

I found his hand under the covers. "Not at all. We'll know when it's time. Just like everything else."

"God," he murmured again. "Yeah. Okay." The last bit was a whisper, and I was pretty sure he was asleep after that.

Loki started purring deeply, and I let that rumble lull me to sleep, too.

CHAPTER 14

JON

I woke up in Drake's apartment as soon as light crept in around the curtains. My shoulder ached if I breathed in the wrong direction, and my head felt like someone had shoved scratchy wool into it, all fuzzy and itchy at the same time. Tears threatened to sneak their way out of my eyes, because I was in bed with Drake, in his apartment, with Loki sleeping between us and Thor curled up on my feet.

He'd opened his place to me. More than that—he was making it my space, too. My cats, my clothes, my laptop—my books, for goodness sake. Even the food that would've spoiled had it been left in the fridge.

Drake had even offered Papa a place to stay.

He wanted to *marry* me.

Maybe it was my soft laugh that woke Drake. "Hey," he said, then he propped himself up on an arm and peered at me, alarm taking over his face. "You okay? Do you need some painkillers?"

"No, no, I'm fine."

"You're crying."

I guess I was. I wiped the tears from my eyes. "Sorry. I think everything has fucked up my emotions and I lost my filter, not that I had much of one, but—I'm just so grateful right now, that's all." My voice wobbled, and I should've hated that. But I didn't. "You brought me my *cats*," I whispered.

Loki stretched out a paw and heaved a very loud sigh.

That let me get my voice back in check. I huffed a laugh. "Oh, are we disturbing his majesty?"

Loki's ear twitched and he flicked his tail.

Drake chuckled. "Of course I brought you your cats."

"I know, but—" There was a lot in my head bumping up against the scratchiness from the anesthesia. Always took a couple days to get all of my brain back on-line. "You think beyond me. I mean, you think about my life."

Drake reached over and cupped my cheek. "You taught me that, Jon. You're the one who taught me to remember what's important."

That wasn't it either, not entirely. "I can't think of the right words. What I want to say. They're just not there." Fucking anesthesia.

"You don't have to think. Not today." He levered himself up. "We have post-op instructions, and a nurse will be here later. Your dad, sooner, I think. I need to go to morning skate, so he'll stay with you."

Morning— "Oh, shit. You have a game tonight." I blinked a few times and the desire to be *there* flooded me. "I wonder if I could..."

"Babe, no," he said firmly. "You absolutely should not go to a hockey game the day after shoulder surgery." He got out of bed and opened the curtains to let in light.

Yeah. He was probably right.

"Your dad said you'd watch together. He hasn't watched a game with you in ages."

I vaguely recalled that from last night. A lot of it was hazy. A lot was still fuzzy at the edges.

"How's the shoulder?"

"Ugh." It ached. Better than right after I was injured, yes, but this was a dull throb I felt when I breathed too hard or moved suddenly. "Hurts. Guess the nerve block wore off."

"Do you want one of the strong pills? Or just ibuprofen?"

I debated, but settled on the ibu, which Drake brought to me, along with a glass of water.

I groaned and got myself upright to take it, then got to my feet. "I'm not spending all day in bed. I need to move." Prove to myself that I could function.

Thor got up, too, and headed over to the windows, hopped up on a table underneath, and peered out. Loki merely stretched out more. "Lazy bones." I gave him a scritch behind the ears.

Drake had a pile of papers in his hands. "There're some exercises you could do."

"My first exercise will be lifting a coffee cup to my mouth."

At that, Drake laughed. "Okay, okay, I'll make you coffee."

He did and I managed to get cleaned up and dressed mostly on my own. It took some doing, since it had been my dominant shoulder that I'd bungled. Using my left hand for a bunch of things was awkward, but doable.

By the time Papa arrived, I was dressed and caffeinated and working my way through some scrambled eggs and an English muffin with jam.

Drake gave me a quick kiss. "I'll be back after practice." Then he was gone, and it was Papa and me in Drake's apartment. I felt like a kid again, and my brain immediately clicked over to Swedish. "He wants to marry me," I blurted out.

Papa's eyebrows rose. "Did he propose?"

"No, I kind of did. But he wants that, too."

Papa burst out laughing. "Kind of?"

I shrugged and told my father what I'd said.

He nodded. "So it goes. Your mother will be happy. Or rather she's happy you've finally found someone. She told me after the first phone call that he'd be our son-in-law."

"How did Mom know?"

Another shrug. "She's smarter than I am, that's for sure." He eyed my English muffin. "Are there more of those?"

There were, and after consuming one, and talking me through my first set of PT exercises, Papa rubbed his hands together. "Sun's shining. I think we have time for a walk before Drake returns, yes?"

Why not? I needed some fresh air, so we went, heading down to Point State Park. We took a stroll around the giant fountain. A cleaning crew was pressure-washing the basin free of the winter muck, but it was still a pleasant walk, with the rivers flowing and the trees budding up.

That's when it hit me. The year was moving on. We were already into spring. I had six to eight months of recovery ahead of me, which meant maybe playing again in October at the earliest, but more than likely, I was missing part of next season, too. Who knew if my shoulder would be the same when I got to the other side of rehab?

I halted and stared out at the confluence of the rivers and the West End bridge beyond. "I'm going to miss the playoffs." I paused. "I might not play again." I didn't know how to feel about *that* thought.

I looked at Papa and found him gazing where I had been. "You'll miss playoffs," he agreed, solemnly. Then he turned to me, his smile mild. "But let's not get ahead of ourselves about your career, yes?"

I didn't know what to say to that. I was nowhere near well enough to even think about stepping on the ice. This slow walk would probably tire me out for the rest of the day.

Papa clapped me on my good shoulder. "Come on." We continued our walk and found our way to a bench on the Allegheny side of the park. My father sat, and I joined him.

"Jon," he said. "You'll be fine, no matter what happens."

"I know, I know. I just—I'd hate that to be my last pro game."

"A game-winning goal in overtime?" He arched an eyebrow.

Okay, when he said it like that, it sounded a lot better than 'tripped over an opponent and broke my shoulder.' I waved a hand in surrender. "That's not so bad." I was tired of being morose about myself, so I switched subjects. "Tell me about your latest charity thing."

Oh, Papa knew what I was doing, but he regaled me with stories from all the charity event he'd been to as we walked back to Drake's apartment. "You and Drake should come up sometime over the summer. Maybe when Sofia is visiting?"

That might be a lot of fun. "I'll have to see what the rehab schedule is like."

Papa waved my concerns away. "We have PT people and trainers in Vancouver. I'm sure your team will be okay with you actually having a summer vacation."

I laughed at that.

When we got back to Drake's, I was grateful to be sitting down again. The fresh air and the movement had been good, but as predicted, fatigue set in quickly. "Ugh, I hate surgery," I muttered.

"Most people do," Papa said cheerfully.

Drake returned and both he and I ended up taking pre-game naps while Papa went out and somehow managed to buy—in downtown Pittsburgh—what he needed to cook dinner for me and him. "We could've ordered something," I said as he unpacked. I stopped and stared at the cloth bag he'd used, which was from Stanley Park. "Did you actually bring a shopping bag with you, all the way from Vancouver?" When I'd been a kid, he'd taken one with him everywhere because "you never know when you need a bag."

My father, the debonair, intelligent man that he was, rolled his eyes at me, "Of course I did."

Drake burst out laughing. "You two are so related," he said. He'd changed into his suit and tie, only lacking the dress shoes.

Thing was, we hadn't been speaking English. "How'd you know what we were saying?"

"I didn't." Drake stole one of the strawberries my dad had bought and ate it. "I know that tone—" he nodded at me "—and that expression," he said, nodded at Papa. Then he glanced at his watch. "I need to head out."

I drew him in for a kiss. "See you later tonight. Have fun. Score a goal for me?"

"Of course."

"Good luck, son," Papa said. "Play well."

Drake's eyes widened, but his smile seemed delighted. "I'll try."

He did more than try. Ended up with two goals and two assists and helped the Lions to a 5-3 victory. It was very strange watching hockey with my father again, and I found that we were making similar observations. "Bad pinch," Papa and I muttered as one of the younger Lions defenders cheated up the boards. And yes, that had led to a two-on-one going the other direction. Luckily, the Lions goalie didn't react too quickly and was able to slide over to make the save. On one of Drake's goals, we both saw the play develop in the defensive zone, and weren't at all surprised when the puck ended up behind the opposing goalie.

"He's rattled," Papa said, regarding the goalie. "Not a good night for him. Too far into the net. Too reactive." I nodded along.

As happy as I was for the win, by the time the game was over, I was yawning uncontrollably. I was practically asleep on the couch (with Loki sleeping on me) by the time Drake returned. He and Papa chatted about the game for a while. The sound was a happy one, and my heart was warm, even if my brain was checked out.

"I should get him to bed," Drake said softly. "Thanks for staying with him today."

"He's my son," Papa said. "There's very little I wouldn't do for him."

"Same," Drake said. "Same."

I guess I didn't have to worry too much about the future. Whatever happened with my injury, Drake would be there, and that was enough.

PAPA FLEW BACK TO VANCOUVER A WEEK LATER, AND A few days after that, I was left to my own devices when Drake headed to New York and Buffalo on a quick two-game road trip. I think he was more worried about me than I was. I couldn't drive, but I'd watched the last two games of the homestand with Papa at the arena. We'd even made it up onto the arena screen—of course because he was Gunner Eriksson, the Hockey Hall of Fame player, not because of me.

What had surprised me (but shouldn't have) was the offers of help from several of the Lions players, partners, and spouses while Drake was away. Gavin, who also lived downtown, offered to run me up to the training center for my physical therapy appointment, and Brodie Boon offered to drive me to Greensburg if I needed to check on my house.

I took both up, after checking to make sure Brodie would be okay with a side-trip to the Hideaway to see how things were going there. Brodie laughed. "Oh hell, yeah. I've been wanting to go to that bar for ages. Oliver was always worried it wouldn't be as trans friendly as people said it was." He shrugged. "If we'd known you owned it..."

"No, I get it."

As it was, Ella, Lorelei, and the rest of the crew were happy to see me, and the pool queens took Brodie under their wings and ended up in a pretty competitive game in the back of the bar.

The books looked fine, Ella was fine. The bar was absolutely *fine*, and I realized that I'd gotten the bar to a spot where it could run without me hovering over it like an overprotective parent.

That was both gratifying and saddening. I'd worked hard to get the bar to where it was, but knowing you weren't needed was its own humbling experience. Felt like... well, it felt like my life right now. I was standing still and everything was moving all around me. Unsettling. Not bad, per se... but I didn't know how I felt about it all.

That wasn't *quite* true.

There was a weight lifted off my shoulders, like I could breathe a little easier. Part of me was relieved that the bar could thrive without me. I'd loved running this place, but now with my recovery and Drake being my priorities, the bar had become less of one.

Red Dog ambled over. "Guess you're not getting on your bike any time soon," he said. "You want me to take it out sometime?"

That wasn't a bad idea. I'd be able to drive in another week or two, but I could *imagine* my orthopedist's look if I asked about riding my motorcycle. "If you'd like, I'd appreciate that." He already had a key to my garage.

Red Dog nodded. "Figured. Shoulders." He rolled his own out. "They're bitches."

They were, and those words came back to me over the weeks afterward.

I spent most of my time at Drake's, since it was closer to rehab and the training center. I'd bullied them into letting me skate—no gear, no stick, low speeds—to get my feet under me. The off-ice rehab picked up. My fucking shoulder really didn't want to do what I wanted it to do—not easily and not fast. "These things take time." That was the gist from my doctors and the PT folks. Even from my parents and Coach Macintosh.

Once I could drive again, I went to as many Otters games as I could manage—I was still the captain and owed it to the team to be there. Plus, it was good to be around the guys, even if they did give me shit about running off to be a hockey husband.

"You gonna dye your hair blond? Brodie asked.

I rolled my eyes and shoved him. "Not every hockey partner is blonde. Oliver, for instance," I said pointedly.

"And the brunet mafia would have my head if I did, anyway."

He cackled.

The Otters were heading to the PHL playoffs. The Lions were heading to the NAPH ones, and I was torn about this turn of events. I was happy for both teams, but I wanted to be in both places—watch both sets of games.

Of course, I chose the Otters. They'd ended up giving Alfie an A, which he admitted to me left him breathless at first, being a rookie and all, but he did well with it. He'd always been a good voice in the locker room.

The Otters games were exciting and intense, and it fucking hurt to watch them from the media box. I helped out where I could, adding my suggestions and observations to the coaches after each game.

But honestly, I didn't need to. They were playing well. So well, that they made it into the semi-final round of the playoffs before finally losing a series.

Sucked, but man, what a run. Next year would be even better, I thought.

Because of my rehab, I couldn't make any of the Otters road trip games, so I did end up watching a few of the Lions playoff games with the other partners and spouses. Unfortunately, the Lions had drawn New York for their first round and while they'd played hard and pushed the series to seven games, they'd fallen in the end. Still, that had been the Lions first trip to the Cup playoffs in a while and Drake's first ever. A good learning experience, everyone said.

Drake wanted more. "Next year," he said, eyes blazing with passion the night after that final loss. "I want to be in the final next year."

Pretty sure he'd will the Lions there, given the fire in him. He'd been instrumental in getting the Lions into the playoffs in the first place. In the end, he'd scored seven playoff goals.

I was also damn sure the only time Drake would ever be in an Otters uniform again would be if—God forbid— he required a conditioning stint. He was well beyond his slump now.

Not sure if it was the Lions or Drake's mother, but that jerkface of a bio dad of his didn't show his electronic face for the rest of the season, not since the birthday message. When Drake had finally told his mom about that incident, she'd been fuming. But that seemed settled, now. I hoped.

Me? Well, I was in the thick of rehab now, working on strengthening my right arm and all those damn muscles in the shoulder. I was also working out the rest of my body, to try to keep it in somewhat decent condition so I wouldn't be a complete disaster when I hit the ice in gear again.

I was skating, but not anything close to the intensity of hockey. That would come in late summer. Maybe. If the doctors deemed my shoulder good enough.

After both teams' playoff hopes had been dashed, Drake and I did travel to Vancouver to spend some time with my parents and sister, and then flew to Philly to spend time with Drake's mom, too.

In the Philly suburbs, after a round of working out with a trainer some of the local NAPHers used, I think Drake caught on that I wasn't exactly my normal upbeat self when we returned to his mom's house. He drew me into the guest room we were occupying. "You all right with being here with my mom?" He had that look of worry he got whenever he was thinking through the worst possible scenario.

I took both of his hands in mine. "I love being here with your mom. She's a wonderful person, and I can see exactly where your strength comes from."

"But..." he said.

"No buts," I said. "None at all."

Ah, there was the skepticism I knew well. "You're not yourself."

I heaved a sigh. "I know. I'm thinking too much. It happens."

"About me?"

I shook my head. "I love you. I want to be with you, and nothing in the world is going to change that. It's—" I gestured to my arm. "It still hurts, Drake. Deep inside. The doctors say it's fine. I'm recovering as planned, but..."

"There's the *but*," he said, and drew me into his arms. "Whatever happens, you'll be fine."

An echo of my father's words. "I know," I said. "I don't like not knowing what 'be fine' is, though. It's..." I opened up space, sat on the bed, and looked up at him. "You know in a game, you can see a couple plays ahead? Well, there's too many plays, and I don't know what route I should take, where I should be, who to pass to. It's all hazy. I know in the end I'll be all right, but don't know what that means or how to get there."

Drake took this in, then sat next to me on the bed. "We're in this together, okay? Whatever you decide, whatever you need, I'll support it." He paused. "You told me that it would all work out as it should if I trusted myself and remembered who I was. I know you'll find the right path—you've done that your entire life. I believe in you."

I didn't say anything, not because there weren't words, but because there were too many and I couldn't squeeze them out. So I pulled Drake into my arms and held him and let my fear of not knowing the future go.

Three words did work their way out of my tangled head

eventually. Ones that were true, ones that wouldn't change. "I love you."

"Know that," he murmured. "Love you, too."

THE TRIP TO THE LIONS TRAINING CENTER HAD become exceedingly routine once I started on ice workouts. There was the off-ice portion, the talk with the team medical staff, and then skating with the skills coach. I appreciated the fact that the Lions were giving me the best care they could, since the Otters were owned by the NAPH team. They weren't leaving me high and dry. They were doing everything they could to get me game-ready.

It was mid-September, and I'd come a hell of a long way over the summer. My shoulder felt better—almost normal. It ached at odd moments or when I moved in unexpected ways. The only issue was that I was a thirty-year-old PHL player with the skills of a PHL player. There wasn't much that could be done to improve that. The Lions skills coach tried, as did their skating coach, and I worked as hard as I ever did.

I can't say I didn't get better—I did—but there was an upper limit. Still, it felt good, putting my body through the paces.

I'd gotten back on my bike, and even taken some rides with Red Dog and his crew. On highways, too. That had been fun. We'd gone to Hideaway after. Everyone at the bar was happy to see me. Felt strange, though. Like I was more of a guest than an owner. I looked over the books, but honestly, I was relieved that everything was in order and I didn't have to do any work.

I wasn't managing the bar, and that felt—fine. Better than my shoulder, in many ways.

I think I found the most solace in the motions of hockey, even if my body wasn't a hundred percent.

As the Lions trickled back to Pittsburgh, a few joined us during those morning sessions, but once more players showed up, they moved on to Capitan's skates, and the training sessions were relegated to the folks like me—rehabbing injuries.

After signing a two-year bridge deal with the Lions, Drake spent part of the summer playing in a local league with other pro players. I wasn't cleared for contact, so I watched him play. Gave some pointers. Then his team pulled me behind the bench to play coach. It was for fun, but it didn't stop anyone from being competitive. Our team ended up winning the cup, which was a monstrosity of a trophy crafted from a thrift-store-bought bowl badly painted with hockey cliches, and held up by a plastic elephant and some GI Joes, all on a small cardboard box spray-painted gold.

Ella, being ever so helpful, printed out the photo from social media of us on the ice with that thing and hung it up —in a frame—in Hideaway. "Jonny, you and Drake are legends now," she'd said.

I shook my head at the memory as I stripped my gear off. Today's rehab and skills session at the rink had been early and an official one, since training camp for the Lions had started. There were several Otters players who'd come up for camp, including Alfie and Smitty. Some of the Lions prospects, who might start down on the Otters, were also there.

It was nice to see everyone, but after the quiet of the early rehab session, the raucous locker room was a bit much, especially since I wouldn't be training with the guys. So I caught Drake's eye, mimicked walking with my fingers, and he nodded.

I'd come back and watch the sessions, but for now, I needed to find some quiet in my head.

The training center wasn't empty—it never was. There were fans and hockey media here to watch camp, and kids here to play or train with their teams, plus all the parents. People ignored me. I was another guy in Lions branded pants and a T-shirt. I looked like any coach, and I was on very few people's autograph list. The most I usually got was "You're Gunner Eriksson's kid!" or more recently, "Oh! You're Drake Williams's boyfriend!"

The former I was used to, and the latter? I liked the latter a lot. I *was* Drake's boyfriend. The other partners and spouses had even bought me a leather jacket with his number patched onto it like a riding club's jacket.

The guys at the bar gave me no end of shit about that, but I loved it. Even wore it out with Red Dog's club.

The training center wasn't that big, and I found myself wandering up one hall, into the main lobby, past a gaggle of small children and their parents, and down another hallway. As I passed an office, something on one of the doors caught my attention. It looked like one of those Wanted posters you saw in Wild West movies, but this was a job posting for coaching jobs. Three of them, in fact. An opening for the center's Learn to Skate program, another for coaching the boys 14U team, and one for the 16U girls team. I glanced over the job requirements, then crossed my arms.

I'd enjoyed "coaching" Drake's summer league team, but real coaching? Could I do something like that?

"You thinking of a career change?" a voice beside me asked.

I jumped a little, but recognized the voice's owner immediately. MaryAnne Charleston had won Olympic gold with Team Canada and lifted the Cup a few times in the women's league. She was older now, with graying auburn hair, and I'd seen her around the rink as the Director of Youth Hockey.

She held up her hands. "Sorry, I didn't mean to startle you. I was just curious."

"No, it's just—I was lost in thought." I gestured at the poster. "I'm not sure I have the qualifications."

She arched her eyebrows. "You're Jon Eriksson. You have the qualifications. You've played in the NAPH and you've spent five years as the captain of the Otters. You helped them behind the bench when they went on their cup run."

Right. That was unusual. Someone knowing me for me. I rubbed the back of my neck. "I suppose?"

"Sorry—" She stuck out her hand. "I'm MaryAnne Charleston."

I shook her hand. "I'm Jon—oh of course you know that. And I watched you play in the Olympics."

She laughed. "Mutual fans, I guess. But yes, you're qualified, and if you ever want to switch careers from a seasoned hockey pro to coaching kids, stop on over. We'd love to have you."

"Oh!" I didn't know what to say. "Thank you. I'll keep that in mind."

From down the hall, a man in a helmet, trainer's pants and a jacket yelled, "Hey Charlie!"

"Ah shit. Gotta go work," she said. "No rest for the wicked." Then she was gone.

I blinked after her and exhaled. Then looked at the poster again. Coaching kids? Huh.

That was still in my mind when I headed back to the Lions practice rink to watch a camp session, and it was still in my mind when the GM of the Lions stepped up to the glass next to me.

When I looked over, I did a double-take, because this man hardly ever came down to ice level to watch the team. He had a perch on a balcony above our heads.

"Jonny," he said.

"Mr. Roth," I answered, as a prickling itched up from my feet. This was important. This day, this moment. I finally felt the game moving at speed, the puck was on the ice, and the plays unfolded before me.

"Wanted to talk to you. You mind coming upstairs?"

In my pocket, my phone vibrated, and I knew without checking—knew with my soul—that it was my agent texting me. "Sure," I said.

When we reached Roth's office, I sat in his guest chair, and he took a seat across from me. "Jonny," he said, "you've been a great asset to the Otters. Your leadership, your mentorship, the way you held that team together. Coach Macintosh speaks highly of you."

I nodded, because I knew what was coming. Like my Papa had said, like Drake had said, everything would be fine. "Thank you, sir."

"I know you still have a couple months of rehab ahead of you, but I wanted to talk to you about this coming season." He fiddled with a pen he had on his desk. "There's no easy way to say this, so I'll just say it. We're not re-signing you to the Otters. You'll finish your rehab, and then you'll be a free agent."

I nodded again, then smiled. "I understand."

His brow furrowed, as if he was confused by my reaction. I suppose he expected anger or disappointment, not—calmness.

"It makes sense," I said. "From your perspective. I'm old, and I count toward the veteran limit. Less players you have to bench, more room for younger guys."

He made a pained noise. "Thirty isn't *old*."

That was true from his perspective, especially since he was in his later fifties. "It's closer to the end of a hockey career than twenty-five."

"Point is, you'll have plenty of options once you've recovered from your injury."

I gave a shrug. "I don't plan to leave the area, but you're correct."

At that, he nodded. "Williams has quite the future here."

"Good." I paused as my phone vibrated with another text. "If that's everything? I think my agent is trying to contact me."

Mr. Roth gave me a nod, rose, and held out his hand. When we shook, he said, "You're a smart man, Jon. You'll land on your feet."

"Thanks. Oh, can I suggest Bruno Doran as Otters Captain? The room respects him, and he's got a good head on his shoulders."

"I'll keep that in mind."

On my way down to the rink, I checked my phone, and yup, there was my agent with several texts and a voice mail, all of which said, more or less, *Call me.*

So I found a conference room that looked out onto the player's parking lot, and called him back. "Hey Jack."

"Jonny, look, I don't want this to blindside you during your recovery, but—"

"The Otters aren't re-signing me?"

"Ah, shit. Roth called you first?"

"I'm at the training center. I had ice-time and rehab this morning, then stuck around to watch Lions camp. Roth found me. Took me to his office to tell me the news."

"You don't sound upset." *He* sounded upset, though.

"That's because I'm not." I ticked off all the reasons they wouldn't re-sign me. "Plus who knows how I'm going to play once I finish all this?"

"Well," he said slowly, "I kind of thought by now you might. You know your body better than anyone."

Yeah, that's what worried me. My shoulder didn't feel quite right. It was better—fine, I suppose. But sometimes it didn't move in ways it could before, not without pain, anyway. "The doctors say it's healing fine. They don't see why I shouldn't recover fully."

There was a snort on the line. "Don't PR me, Jonny. What's actually going on?"

"I don't know. It doesn't feel right. I've told them, and they're not concerned, since I can do the exercises and move and all that. Imaging says I should be fine."

He grunted. "Let's keep that to ourselves for now. You could improve in the next few months. I'll start looking—"

I cut him off. "Jack, I'm retiring."

Dead silence, then "What?"

"I'm retiring," I repeated. "Don't waste your time."

"You're *thirty*, Jon. You have *at least* another five years of a pro career. Probably more. The shoulder is just a minor setback" He sounded incredulous. "You can't retire!"

"I can and I am. If I want to keep playing, I'll have to leave western Pennsylvania, and I'm not leaving." My life was here. Drake was here. My bar, my friends. Everything. "It's fine, Jack."

He sputtered on the other end. "Is this your boyfriend's doing?"

I laughed, loudly enough that someone came down the hall and looked into the room—one of the trainers—I waved him off. "*No.*" I paused, then went on. "Oh my God, Jack. You've known me since I was *fourteen*. When has anyone ever made me do *any*thing? Even my father doesn't try. Drake doesn't even know I'm retiring yet." I gestured to the ice, even though Jack couldn't see. "He's still out there training. I haven't talked to him."

Silence on the other end. "Well, you should. It's a big life decision, and if you're serious about him—"

"I am."

He made an annoyed little grunt. "If you're serious about him, you shouldn't make a life-altering decision without him knowing. I'll leave the door open for you. Text me in a week."

I sighed. "All right. But I'll still be retiring in a week."

"Jonny, trust me on this. I do actually have your best interests at heart."

I was sure of that, and appreciated Jack telling me to slow down and not be foolish about this. I also knew Drake and myself, and I'd already pivoted, just like on the ice. The difference was in this, I had the skills to execute this move beautifully. "I know you're looking out for me. I'll talk to you in a week."

We hung up, and I went back to watching the Lions run through drills, seeing each player's strengths and weaknesses. Noting what they needed to work on—all the stuff I used to do in our practices between drills.

I wasn't a hockey player anymore. Sure, Jack would pester me to not retire, but it was official in my head. I always expected when this day came, I'd feel sad, or melancholy, or some negative emotion. Instead, I was excited. Elated. Happy for the future.

Coaching young hockey players? Yes. Bring it on.

Of course, I had to get hired first, but given what Mary-Anne had said, that would happen if I applied. Coaching kids seemed like a useful outlet for a hockey boyfriend. Would keep me out of trouble when Drake was on the road.

I huffed a laugh at myself. Yeah. I *really* did need to talk to Drake.

CHAPTER 15

DRAKE

When I finally made it into the players' lounge after the post-training media scrum, a small workout, and cleaning myself up, Jon was there, chatting with Alfie and some of the other Otters guys. He was loose and smiling—glowing really—in a way he hadn't been in a while. Mr. Sunshine was back. He must've finally gotten the news we'd been waiting for about his next contract.

"Hey," I said, and wrapped my arm around his waist. "You're exceptionally happy."

"He's always happy," Alfie said. "Like summer."

No one was happy *all* the time, though Jon came close. The last couple of weeks, he'd been moody. More contemplative than usual. "I saw JR with you at one point. Did he finally re-sign you?"

Jon huffed a laugh. "No," he said softly. But his smile—he didn't look like someone who'd gotten bad news.

"Bet his agent's still negotiating, and JR's playing hard-ball," Gavin said.

That got another laugh from Jon, and I studied him.

There was something he wasn't saying. I didn't think he was keeping anything—oh shit.

Jon wouldn't tell me he wasn't re-signed in front of a bunch of people. He'd want to talk about it in private. But— I wasn't imagining the way he was relaxed, or how his eyes sparkled with excitement. I gave him a gentle squeeze and matched his smile.

"I met MaryAnne Charleston when I was walking around. I knew she was a director here, but..." He waved his hand. "Olympic gold! Mom was so happy when she won. I can't wait to tell her I've met her."

That might explain the mood. "You talked?"

He shrugged. "Briefly. The Help Wanted poster they had up for coaches caught my eye."

Oh. Then my brain caught up. *Oh.*

Maybe I looked too sharply at him, because that grin widened. "You were right," he said. "You and my father."

That everything would work out. I stared at him. "Yeah?"

And there was all the sparkle and light I hadn't seen since he'd broken his shoulder. "Yeah."

Alfie chuckled. "Wow." He grabbed Gavin's arm. "Come on, let's leave them alone for a couple minutes."

Gavin's brow furrowed. "Why?"

"Because," Alfie said, "they have things to say." He led Gavin away.

"Oh man," Jon said. "Alfie's *smart.*"

"Yeah." I watched his back for a moment, then faced Jon. "JR isn't re-signing you."

"No," he said mildly. "He's not. I'm retiring."

"You're... what?" He was only thirty. I couldn't imagine retiring at thirty.

The lounge got really quiet. Probably because I'd been very loud.

Then Jon laughed and broke all the tension. He threw his arm around my shoulder. "Come on, let's take a walk."

We went to the players' parking lot. "You can't retire."

"Oh, I can," he said, beaming at me. "Look, I don't want to play anywhere else. I want to be with you, so I'm not leaving. If I'm not leaving, I'm retiring. Simple."

"Jon, I can't ask you to—"

"Will you marry me?"

My head swam. What even was happening here? "Yes," I said, since we'd talked about that before. Then I pieced together what he was saying. "Wait. You'd rather marry me than play hockey? But you love hockey!"

"I love you more," he said simply. "And MaryAnne is looking for coaches."

"Hold up." I rubbed my forehead, because my brain hurt from the whirlwind of information and emotions whipping around inside it. Jon loved me more than playing hockey. He wanted to marry me. "Did you just propose?"

He blinked and tilted his head. "I guess I did. I kind of want to be a hockey husband." His laugh seemed to fill the parking lot.

"And a coach."

"I think I'd have fun with it, and I'd still get to skate and handle the puck and all that. Maybe I'll join a rec team or sub in or something, once the shoulder isn't so cranky." He shrugged. "My agent said I should talk to you before I made any big decisions, but it's the *right thing*, Drake."

"What about the bar?"

A little of the sunshine fell into seriousness. "I'll have to talk to Ella first, of course, but she's been running Hideaway while I've been rehabbing. I bet—I hope—she wouldn't mind partnering with me. We'll see. I hate admitting this, but it's been nice not being in charge all the time, and they don't actually need me that much—it's mostly that I stabilize the place, you know? Money-wise. Margins are always close. It's been in the black for a while, but when it wasn't I —" He waved a hand.

"Paid the difference?" Because he could. And he would've to keep the staff on and the community there safe.

"It's—I could do that, so I did. Point is, I can be more of a silent partner."

"You? *Silent*?"

He gave me a gently shove. "You said yes to marrying me."

"I did." God, he was so beautiful like this. Playful. Happy. Looking to the future. "Talk to Ella, then to Mary-Anne. I think it's a good plan. I bet kids are going to love you as a coach."

He grinned at that. "Should we go in and tell the guys I'm retiring and marrying you?"

That was bound to turn the lounge into a madhouse. "Bet you no one had that on their bingo card. Not together."

"Eh, you never know..."

This time I was the one to laugh. We walked back into the facility, arms wrapped around each other, joy in our hearts.

One Year Later

Whenever we stepped into Target, I lost Jon. One moment, he was by my side, the next... vanished. Poof. He'd usually reappear with something absolutely ridiculous. One time, it was a giant squishable pillow in the shape of a lion.

Another, it was a shower curtain with cute otters holding hands.

The perils of buying a house together, I guess. We'd swapped back and forth between our homes last year, but with Jon's coaching job, we'd ended up in Pittsburgh most of the time. Ella had full run of Hideaway, now, so there was no need to return to Greensburg that often. So Jon had sold his house near the woods. Together, we'd bought another house north of Pittsburgh that backed up against a protected nature area that had a stream with rocks for Jon to sit on. Lots of walking and hiking, too. The area even had back roads for Jon to ride his bike on when the weather was good.

After some renovations and painting, we were finally moving into our new place.

But once more, Jon had disappeared during a Target run. Tonight, he reappeared wearing a flower wreath on his head and another in his hand. "It's midsummer!" He set the wreath down on my head.

"This isn't going to turn into some horror movie with a human sacrifice, right?"

Pretty sure the rest of the store heard his laugh. "No, no. It's a party with food and flowers and games. No weird rituals that involve blood or unsuspecting tourists." He peered into the cart. "We should get cookies." He paused. "We should go to IKEA!"

Oh God. Ever since we moved into our new home, that place was like letting Jon loose in a funhouse. I didn't want to admit it, but I was getting tired of meatballs. "We should go to the house and unpack more before the cats decide the stacks of boxes are their new cat trees."

He snorted. "Before?"

I had to laugh at that. "Come on, let's get the stuff we

need and get out of here." Before he found something else, like rainbow His and His T-shirts or something.

"All right. But I'm getting cookies."

I left the flower crown on, gave in, and steered us to the cookie aisle, which was, of course, when one of his players found us.

"Hey, Coach Erik!" The young woman had dark brown hair tied back in a ponytail and was wearing shorts and a Lions Hockey T-shirt. She peered up at his head and had one of those expressions teens got when they think adults are acting weird. "Wow. I like the flowers."

"Midsummer," he said. "It's a Swedish thing. Flowers and food and fun."

I hung back, leaning on the handle of the cart. I loved watching Jon interact with the kids he coached. The 16U team had won their championship under him last season. They'd start up again soon. There were some hockey clinics coming up that Jon would be a part of—and apparently, so would this kid, since she was animatedly telling him about the new gear she'd gotten. "Dad even let me get new skates."

"You bake them?" Jon asked.

"Nivisha?" A man—obviously her dad—rounded the aisle. His hair was graying, but they shared the same South Asian complexion. He was dressed very dad-like in a white polo, dark blue shorts and boat shoes.

"Dad, it's Coach Erik!"

He eyed Jon's crown, glanced at me, then did a double take, his eyes widening. Then he focused back on Jon, who promptly stuck out his hand. "Nice to see you, Mr. Gupta. Nivisha was telling me you got her new gear for the upcoming season?"

That led to a conversation about the price of equipment, but how much Nivisha loved hockey and how he wanted her to have the best so she could play the best.

Finally, Nivisha noticed me with the cart and the matching flower crown. "Hey Mr. Williams." She turned to her dad. "That's Drake Williams. He's Coach Erik's fiancé. He plays for the Lions."

"I know who Drake Williams is," her dad said, sounding a bit put out by his daughter's assumptions. "I watched most of the games last year." He held out his hand, and I shook it. "An honor to meet you."

"Thanks. I'm just along to push the cart." I was still getting used to being Drake Williams, the goal scoring magician. The Lions had ended the season second in our division, and had made it to the semi-finals. We'd pushed this year's eventual Cup winner to seven games and had lost in a heartbreaker of a double overtime game. I'd scored thirty-one goals during the regular season and twelve during our playoff run.

I'd also finally put everything with my bio-father to bed. After leaving me alone for a while, he'd had the audacity to show up and try to get into a closed practice during the playoffs. The fight with security by the door to the practice arena had caught everyone's attention, including Jon. He'd been sitting in the stands. That was the only time I'd ever seen Jon dangerously angry, so I knew I had to do something about it.

By the time I'd gotten out there, security had him under control and the police were on their way. He was a tall man, but in skates, I was taller, and I think that's what caused him to shrink back. Maybe he'd still had the impression I was a little kid, despite being twenty-three.

"You're Drake?" he croaked.

"Yup. And you're the guy who thinks I'm a fucking ATM."

"I'm your dad."

"I don't have a dad. I've never had a dad. You're the guy who had a one-night stand with my mom, then called her a whore and tried to get her to abort me."

The crowd around us murmured.

I stepped up to him, and he backed into the security guard. "You signed away your rights when I was born. 'Washed your hands of me,' isn't that what the email you sent said?"

"Yeah, but—"

"But nothing. My mom worked her ass off to feed and clothe us, and sacrificed so much to get me here." I gestured around the practice facility. "The only reason you're here is because you're looking for a payout. You're not getting it, you useless leech."

His face had gone red, and I think he realized that the people around him were not at all on his side. There were employees, parents, older teens, even some of the hockey reporters with their phones out, recording.

"You've been harassing me this whole year. I told you to stop. Mom told you to stop. Guess now we have to get lawyers and the police involved, huh?" And as if on cue, the local cops walked in.

I nodded to them, then marched back into the arena. The team trespassed him and banned him from their properties, and I filed a restraining order. That—and the articles that came out about the incident—seemed to have scared him off, thank God.

I shook myself out of the memory. Jon was still chatting with Nivisha and her father. "We moved recently. Seems like every time we turn around, we're missing something."

He waved a hand. "Look at me rambling on. I should let you and your daughter go. Niv, work on your shot, eh?"

She rolled her eyes. "Wait until you see my backhand." She pulled her dad down the aisle in the opposite direction.

Jon called after her, "Can't wait!" Then he grabbed a bag of chocolate chip cookies off the shelf. "Just here to push the cart?" He cocked an eyebrow.

"Oh," I said, breezily, "And other things."

There was the bit of pink on his cheeks that I loved so much, along with the grin that matched the summer sun. "Let's go home, and you can tell me all about the other things."

I snorted, pushed the cart, and headed toward the front of the store.

Never in a million years at the start of that fateful season that had sent me to the Otters, had I expected my life to turn out like this.

I was a hockey star—an actual one now. With my likeness on banners and commemorative cups at the arena. I was also pushing a cart through a Target with a crown of flowers on my head.

With a stellar season behind me, and only a year left on my bridge deal, this summer I'd signed a new eight-year contract with the Lions that amounted to more money than I could wrap my head around.

Despite all that, it wasn't me that was turning heads as we walked through Target, it was the dark-haired beautiful man walking next to me. The one who lit up a room, cackled like a madman, and was able to corral a whole team of young women, unlock the game of hockey for them, and lead them to a championship. The man I'd marry next month in front of my mom and his parents, and our friends and teammates.

Getting sent down to the Otters had been the best thing that ever happened to me. I didn't know where I'd be without Jon. Definitely not at a self-checkout at a Target, having him pluck a flower wreath off my head. I could only laugh, as it got tangled in my hair.

"Your damn curls," he said, sighing dramatically.

"You love my damn curls!"

Oh, he softened at that. "I love everything about you," he said, then cocked his head. "Well, almost everything."

I gave him a *look*.

"Socks. Put them in the hamper! That's why it's *there*."

I just snorted, paid for our things, and headed for the exit. "You know I leave them in the living room to annoy you."

"I have Loki to annoy me," he quipped.

My best buddy. Loki had very much claimed me as his person. "You have me to love you."

God, I adored doing that—making Jon stop in his tracks and get that dopy smile of his.

Then he met my gaze. "I have you. I love you. Let's get out of here."

We stepped out into the bright, hot afternoon, and I couldn't help my grin. Jon might've ended up a hockey husband, but I was pretty sure it was me who was about to marry the superstar.

I wouldn't have it any other way.

The End

THANK YOU FOR READING

Dear Reader,

Thank you for reading *Love of the Game*! I hope you enjoyed Drake and Jon's story as much as I enjoyed writing it.

There are plenty more books in *The Games We Play* series, so check them out. They're all listed following this.

If you enjoyed *Love of the Game*, and want to read additional hockey romances by me, I've co-written *Rookie Mistake* and *Scoreless Game* with L.A. Witt. They have a lot more angst in them than this book, but also the warm team dynamics and fun found here.

To find out more about my books and new releases, you can follow me on BookBub, join my facebook group or sign up for my newsletter.

Thank you so much!

-Anna

GAMES WE PLAY SERIES

ALSO BY ANNA ZABO

TAKEOVER

Takeover

Just Business

Due Diligence

Daily Grind

ON THE BOARD (WRITTEN WITH L.A. WITT)

Rookie Mistake

Scoreless Game

Shift Change (coming soon)

TWISTED WISHES

Syncopation

Counterpoint

Reverb

CLOSE QUARTER

Close Quarter

Slow Waltz (a Close Quarter short story)

STANDALONE WORKS

CTRL Me

Outside the Lines

Weave the Dark, Weave the Light

Cinnamon Roll

Love of the Game

ABOUT THE AUTHOR

Anna Zabo writes contemporary and paranormal romance for all colors of the rainbow. They live and work in Pittsburgh, Pennsylvania, which isn't nearly as boring as most people think.

They can be easily plied with coffee or a chance to see the Pittsburgh Penguins.

Anna has an MFA in Writing Popular Fiction from Seton Hill University, where they fell in with a roving band of romance writers and never looked back. They also have a BA in Creative Writing from Carnegie Mellon University.

Anna uses they/them pronouns and prefers Mx. Zabo as an honorific. They can be found online at annazabo.com.

𝕏 x.com/amergina

 instagram.com/amergina

BB bookbub.com/authors/anna-zabo

a amazon.com/Anna-Zabo/e/B00A7LA6OC

www.ingramcontent.com/pod-product-compliance
Lightning Source LLC
Chambersburg PA
CBHW030143200626
46812CB00015B/925